Longarm plunged down
into blackness . . .

For a moment he lay without moving, then full consciousness flooded back, but the darkness did not abate. Slowly he lifted himself to his feet.

By the dim reddish light of a flickering match, he examined the hole through which he had fallen. It was far above his head, at least four or five feet, well out of reach. As the match flickered and began to burn his fingertips, Longarm belatedly looked around the underground chamber, and by the match's dying flame got a glimpse of a number of oblong bundles laid in neat rows on the floor . . .

. . . the bodies of dead men wrapped in some kind of rough cloth.

TABOR EVANS

LONGARM

AND THE
GREAT CATTLE KILL

A JOVE BOOK

LONGARM AND THE GREAT CATTLE KILL

A Jove Book/published by arrangement with
the author

PRINTING HISTORY
Jove edition/July 1986

ISBN: 0-515-08607-X

PRINTED IN THE UNITED STATES OF AMERICA

Chapter 1

An alien noise breaking the silence in the midnight-dark room brought Longarm instantly awake. He reached for the Colt that always lay within reach of his hand on the chair beside his bed at night, but his fingers found only empty air.

Longarm's move had been instinctive, the quick response of a man who lived on the brink of danger. A second after his hand had groped in vain for his revolver, reason took over from instinct. He realized now that he was not in his own room, his own bed, and that he was not alone.

Even before the woman lying beside him stirred and sighed as his movement roused her from sleep, Longarm realized where he was. With realization came the awareness that he had not been roused by a threat of danger, but by some unconscious move or noise made by his bedmate. As he relaxed and settled back on his pillow, his companion's voice broke the stillness of the curtained room.

"Did I wake you up?" she asked. Her hand snaked slowly

1

up his chest, and she ran her warm, soft fingertips through the brush of stiff curls on his chest.

"Sure looks like you did," he told her.

"I guess I'm a little bit nervous," she said. "It's been quite a while since I've had a man in bed with me. Maybe I was dreaming about what I've got to face tomorrow . . . today, now, I suppose . . . and it made me restless."

"Well, it don't make much of a never-mind why you woke up, Janis," Longarm replied. "Come right down to it, I'm sorta glad you did."

"Let's be glad together," Janis suggested. "I'm glad you were gentleman enough to stop and help me when that porter in the Kansas City depot was so insolent. If he'd been polite, you never would have stopped. Then we'd have ridden here to Denver on the same train as strangers, and we wouldn't be here right now."

Janis had drawn Longarm's attention in Kansas City the previous day. She had stopped in the door of the Union Depot and was blocking the way to the train while she tried to get the porter carrying her bags to move faster. As a regular and observant traveller, Longarm had recognized the man's slow movements as a common trick employed by some porters to make passengers anxious and force them to promise an extra tip for speeding up.

Longarm had solved the problem for Janis in two seconds. He rested his big, muscular hand on the porter's shoulder and tightened it firmly. His voice low but hard, he had said, "This lady's in a hurry to get to her train before it pulls out and it's your job to see that she's not late. Now, suppose you do what you're supposed to before I decide to help her myself and do you out of a tip."

A single brief glance at Longarm's steely blue-grey eyes convinced the porter he would be wise to obey. He nodded and said to Janis, "Don't you get worried, lady. I'll get you to your coach on time."

Her face still fixed in a worried frown, Janis had given Longarm a nod of thanks as she hurried past him through the door. Later, as the train chugged across the flatlands and began the long climb up toward the Rockies, Longarm had seen her sitting alone at a table in the dining car. She had caught his eye and nodded an invitation for him to join her.

Longarm doffed his hat and made a half-bow, his eyes flick-

2

ing over her with a quick glance. He saw a woman in her mid-thirties with dark blond hair, brown eyes, and an aquiline nose. She had full, pouting lips, and, from the bulges in the jacket of her neat grey twill travelling suit, an interestingly full figure. Her smooth white hands and manicured nails indicated that she belonged to the class that did no household work, while the pearl-bordered cameo on her blouse and the large but not showy diamond on her left ring finger indicated that she was not rich, but quite well off.

"I didn't stop to thank you for speaking to that porter," she had said. "I was too worried about getting to the train."

"Why, I don't look for thanks just for setting a man straight about his job," Longarm replied. "But I'm glad I was on hand where I could help you."

"My name's Janis Treadwell," she went on. "And this is the farthest west I've ever been."

"I'm Custis Long, ma'am. If you need any more help, just feel free to call on me."

"I'm not usually nervous about travelling." Janis frowned. "This trip is an exception, though. I'm sure I'll feel better when I get to Denver and finish the unpleasant business that's waiting for me there."

"It sounds to me like you ain't real glad to be making this trip," Longarm suggested.

"I'm not," she agreed. "But I'll—"

Whatever Janis was going to say had been lost then as the dining-car waiter came to take their order. She made no effort to pick up the conversation after the man left. It was not until later, after they had finished eating and she had invited Longarm to share her seat in the passenger coach, that she allowed their talk to become more personal.

"As I told you, Mr. Long, this is the first time I've ever been to Denver," she had said. "But I suppose you live there?"

"About as much as I live anyplace," he had replied.

"You travel a lot, then?"

"Pretty much."

"That's not what I expected you to say." Janis had frowned. She looked at Longarm's polished boots, tan covert-cloth trousers, and long black coat. "From the way you're dressed, I'd have taken you for a stockman or a rancher."

"Well, I did some cowpunching for a little while, when I struck out on my own, but I never got enough money together to set myself up on a spread," he had confessed. "No, I ain't rich or important. Just a deputy United States marshal."

"That sounds important to me. Goodness, I feel safer already, just having you sit with me, Mr. Long. Or should I call you Marshal Long?"

"Why, you can suit yourself about that, Miz Treadwell. But I got a sorta nickname my friends call me by, and I answer to it a lot easier than I do to mister or marshal. It's Longarm."

Janis Treadwell smiled. "Of course! The long arm of the law. Very well, Longarm. And you must call me Janis."

"It'll be a lot friendlier that way," Longarm nodded. "And if there's any way I can help you while you're in Denver, you'll find me at the federal building, on the second floor."

Janis was silent for a moment before she replied, "There's one way you can help me right now. I don't know of any hotel in Denver."

"Maybe you'd like the Windsor," Longarm suggested. "It ain't very fancy or expensive, but it's real nice and comfortable."

"I'll rely on your recommendation, then," she nodded. "And now tell me about your adventures as a U.S. marshal."

"Well, mostly it's about like any other job a man works at. Like this trip I'm just going back from—I had to take a couple of crooks to the new federal pen at Fort Leavenworth. They acted all right, didn't give me no trouble, so all I did was take a ride on the train."

Janis was briefly silent again. Then she said, "It's funny in a way, I suppose, but my trip to Denver is just the opposite of going to jail. After I get through with my business there, I'll feel like I'm just getting out of jail. You see, I'm going there for a divorce trial. My husband and I separated several years ago, and I lost track of him until recently. He's living in Denver now, so I filed for a divorce in Colorado."

"Well, now, I'm sorry to hear that."

"Don't be. I'll be very glad to be rid of him. As soon as I found out where he was, I went to a lawyer and he arranged for the divorce case. My husband's been making me a good allowance since I ran him to earth, and I'm counting on him continuing it until I settle down, maybe find a good husband." She shook her head, smiled wryly, and went on, "Now, let's forget such unpleasant things and talk about something else."

For the remainder of the trip, Longarm and Janis Treadwell

4

had talked of impersonal things. When they arrived in Denver, Longarm had volunteered to escort her to the hotel, and while the brief formalities of registration were being completed had started to ask Janis to have dinner with him.

Before he could frame his invitation, she had surprised him by saying, "Longarm, I'm going to ask another favor of you. I don't look forward to going into the restaurant for dinner, and I don't feel like eating alone. Will you have dinner with me in my room?"

Longarm showed no surprise. While he hadn't expected Janis's invitation, he'd received enough like it in the past to keep his face from showing any reaction. Nor had he been surprised later, when as soon as the waiter had left after bringing up their dinner, Janis did not move to sit down at once, but turned away from the gleaming china- and silver-set table to face him.

"Are you very hungry, Longarm?" she asked. "Because if you're not, I can think of something much more pleasant to do right now than just having a meal together."

"I was just thinking along those lines myself," Longarm had answered. "And I'm ready whenever you are."

Now, with the still untouched food cold on the table across the room, Janis snuggled up closer to Longarm and slid her soft, warm thigh across his legs. Her head resting on his shoulder, she stroked her fingers through his wiry chest curls, across his flat stomach, and down still further until she reached his groin. Their eyes had already adjusted to the dim glow that came through the drawn shades from the streetlights outside, and Longarm looked down at Janis to see a smile grow on her face.

"Maybe I woke up because I was dreaming about you," she whispered. "Dreaming how it was before we went to sleep."

"We sure ain't sleeping now."

He raised himself on one elbow, then bent down to find Janis's warm soft lips. Janis responded with a throaty sigh that soon became a yearning moan, and her body started to quiver. Janis inched further over onto him, her thighs spreading wider. Breaking their kiss, she asked, "Do you mind if I get on top and ride you this time?"

"If that's what'll pleasure you," Longarm replied.

Longarm lay back, one of his big hands on each of Janis's breasts. Raising his head, he began kissing the soft billows in turn, rasping his tongue over their pebbled rosettes and protruding tips.

Janis's sighs were becoming louder now. Her quivering had turned into a series of jerks that twisted her entire body. She lifted herself suddenly and sank down in a quick move that ended in a throaty cry of pleasure.

"Oh, Longarm!" she gasped as she brought her body upright and wriggled slowly from side to side, her eyes half closed. "I think dreaming about doing this is what woke me up a minute ago."

"Go on and enjoy it," Longarm advised. "If it'll make you feel better, I sorta like it, too." He grasped her hips, one big hand on each side, and pulled her down to press against him more firmly.

Janis was beginning to gasp now. Her head was thrown back, her eyes closed, her full lips twisting as she rocked faster and faster. The moans that had been bubbling from her lips grew louder. Then she screamed ecstatically, head thrown back, as she exploded into a frenzy of twisting and wriggling that ended in a throaty sigh of satisfaction. She slumped forward on Longarm's chest, her head cradled on his muscular shoulder.

For a long while they lay silent; then Longarm lifted himself away from her. "I guess I better say good night before we get started off again," he told her regretfully.

"Don't go," she pleaded. "I'm exhausted, but that doesn't mean we can't sleep quietly together for the rest of the night."

"There ain't a thing in the world I'd like better, Janis," Longarm said soberly. "But I'm thinking about you. On the train you said your lawyer couldn't be here until tomorrow, so I don't guess your husband's lawyer looks for you to be here until then."

"I don't understand what you're trying to say," she told him, a frown growing on her face.

"Why, I'm thinking about your husband's lawyer. I know how them jackleg divorce fellows work. It's a fifty-to-one bet that they got some private detective ready to watch the trains coming in from the East tomorrow, all primed to spy on you."

"They can't watch me if I'm not *on* a train," she said.

"No, but if you don't come on the same train with your lawyer they'll figure pretty fast you must've got in tonight. It wouldn't take them long to find out you were here at the Windsor, and there ain't no secrets in hotels that a ten-dollar

6

gold piece won't buy from a clerk or waiter or chambermaid."

"I see what you're getting at." Janis nodded slowly. "If they could prove I spent the night with you, they'd be able to claim I'm a loose woman, and I'd be out in the cold."

"That's about what I was trying to say, the best way I could figure to," Longarm agreed.

"But I will see you again before I leave, won't I?"

"You sure will, if I got anything to say about it," Longarm promised. He finished buttoning his grey flannel shirt and stepped into his trousers. "But I ain't my own boss, you know. There might be some kind of case waiting that my chief'd send me out on right away."

"How will I find you, then?" she asked.

"Just send me a little note to the U.S. Marshal's office in the federal building. Then I'll come in a hurry and find you," he promised.

"All right," Janis nodded. "And, Longarm . . ." She hesitated for a moment. "Thanks for helping me find out I'm a full woman again."

"Now, that's something you don't need to worry about," he assured her. Stepping to the bed, he bent over Janis for a quick goodbye kiss, and let himself out of the room.

As he walked through the Windsor's vast ornate lobby, deserted at this hour of the morning, Longarm could see the white flakes of a late spring snowfall swirling in the outside air. He emerged into a night that had suddenly become wintry. An inch or more of snow covered Denver's streets. Swooping down from the slopes of the Rockies, the thin cold wind that had brought the snow cut through Longarm's coat and trousers.

You know, old son, he told himself as he stopped on the sidewalk to light one of his long thin cigars, *this damn Rocky Mountain weather's just like a woman that can't make up her mind whether to say yes or no, whether to hold on or let go. But it's a long walk home, and you better treat yourself to a hackney.*

Twenty minutes later Longarm paid the cabby and mounted the narrow stairs to his second-floor room. Flicking an iron-hard thumbnail across a match head, he lifted the chimney of the kerosene lamp that stood on a scarred three-drawer bureau and touched the match to its wick. The room's faded wallpaper, sagging bed, thin threadbare rug, and tattered window shades were a sharp contrast to the luxurious room he had just left, but Longarm felt more at home in it than he had in the hotel room.

Levering out of his flat-heeled cavalry boots, he padded barefoot to the corner curtained off as a closet and hung his long-skirted coat on one of the hooks. Unbuckling his gunbelt, he laid the holstered Colt in the chair standing at the head of the bed. He took his stubby .44 derringer out of his vest pocket, bringing with it the watch to which the weapon was attached by the watch chain.

He placed these on the edge of the chair near the Colt before taking off his vest and hanging it over the back of the chair, where the pocket holding his cigars would be within easy reach. Finally, he skinned out of his trousers and underwear at the same time and hung them on the bedpost.

Stretching and yawning, Longarm threw back the threadbare bedspread and stepped over to the bureau to blow out the lamp. The bottle of Tom Moore on the bureau caught his eye and he tilted it to his lips for a nightcap before puffing down the lamp chimney to extinguish the wick.

In the dark room, he stepped to the bed and sat down, his hand by force of habit reaching to the pocket of his vest for a cigar. Before his fingers closed over one of the long, thin cheroots, he thought better of it and fell back on the creaking springs. Pulling the bedspread over his shoulders, he was fast asleep within two minutes.

Chapter 2

Longarm was still sleeping soundly when a pounding on the door of his room brought him bolt upright in bed. Dawnlight was showing around the edges of the tattered window shades. Though he could tell that the sun was not yet up, the light brightened the room more than usual because it was reflected from the snow that had sifted down during the night.

He tossed aside the cover with one hand and started to roll from the bed. Longarm's free hand swept down to the chair and grabbed the butt of his Colt. The loud knocking was repeated as he swung his feet to the floor and padded barefoot to the door. Standing at one side of the thin panels, Longarm waited for the third series of knocks before replying.

"Who's there and what do you want?" he asked, raising his voice a bit.

A man's light voice responded, "It's just me, Marshal Long."

Longarm recognized the voice at once; it was that of Henry, Billy Vail's clerk.

Jerking the door open, Longarm asked, "What in tunket are you doing rousing me outa bed at this time of day? It's Sunday morning, damn it, and I ain't even due to go to the office!"

"It wasn't my idea to get you out of bed," Henry said quickly, his jaw dropping when he saw Longarm standing naked in the open doorway, the Colt dangling from his hand.

"I guess it wasn't, at that," Longarm replied, his temper losing its edge. "Well, come on in. You can tell me what this is all about while I get my clothes on."

"I wish I could tell you, Marshal Long, but I don't know any more than you do," the clerk said. He came into the room and Longarm closed the door.

"Then just don't talk to me about a thing till I have a swallow of Tom Moore to clear the cobwebs away," Longarm told him. He stepped over to the bureau and picked up the half-empty bottle of Moore, pulled the cork, and downed two sizeable swallows. As he lowered the bottle of Maryland rye, he belatedly realized his involuntary role as host and extended the bottle to the clerk. "Maybe you'd enjoy a sip yourself."

"That's very kind of you, Marshal Long," Henry said quickly. "But I wear the white ribbon."

"Temperance, are you?" Longarm said. He swallowed another gulp of the pungent rye and nodded. "You know, I oughta figured that out before I offered."

"Oh, no offense taken, Marshal. But I'd appreciate it if you'd get ready to go downtown. Chief Marshal Vail is really anxious to see you as soon as possible."

"I guess it's got to be important," Longarm said. He put the bottle back on the bureau and stepped to the chair where his clothing was hanging. He fished a long, thin cigar from the pocket of his vest and lighted it, then through a cloud of smoke went on, "If it wasn't something that Billy needed to get done right away, he wouldn't've got you down to the office just to come out here and roust me out."

"That's not exactly how it happened," the clerk said, frowning. "The chief marshal didn't call me to the office. I just stopped by on my way to church to pick up a present I bought for my girl. I forgot to take it home when I left last night. It's her birthday, you see, and I want to give it to her when I meet her to go to Sunday school."

Longarm had his balbriggans and shirt on by now and was

stepping into his trousers. "Are you telling me that Billy put you to work on Sunday, just like that?" he asked.

"Just like that." Henry nodded. "He said he knew I wasn't supposed to work Sundays, and to save my time as much as possible he gave me the money to take a hackney carriage out here and said I could have the cabby take me on to church."

"And he figures that I'll walk to the office, I guess?" Longarm asked over his shoulder. He was standing at the bureau tying his black string tie.

"He didn't say anything about that, Marshal Long. But I've done the errand, like he told me to, so I'll just excuse myself and go about my own business."

"Whoa, now!" Longarm exclaimed. "Just you stand still while I finish dressing." He restored his derringer and watch to their pockets and reached for his gunbelt.

"Now, Marshal Long, Chief Marshal Vail didn't say a word about me using that hackney carriage to take you downtown to the office. If I do that, he's liable to get mad at me."

"If Billy Vail objects, you just refer him to me, and I'll stand ready to take the blame."

"Now that I think about it, I don't imagine the chief marshal would object, at that," the clerk responded. "He's in a mighty big hurry to get you there. I could see that from the way he acted."

"By himself, was he?" Longarm asked, shrugging into his coat.

"As a matter of fact, he wasn't, Marshal Long. Chief Marshal Vail was sitting in his private office at his desk, and there was a man with him, but all I could see was his feet."

"I'll find out what's going on soon enough, I suppose," Longarm said, taking his hat off its hook and settling it on his head. "I guess I'm as ready as I'll ever be, so let's get cracking."

"Do you think I ought to go upstairs to the office with you when we get to the federal building?" Henry asked as he and Longarm descended the stairs.

Longarm blinked when the reflected light of the rising sun shining on the new-fallen snow hit his eyes. He did not reply to the clerk's question until they had settled down on the seat of the hackney cab.

"Did Billy say he wanted you to come back?" Longarm asked. When the clerk shook his head, he went on, "Don't go

11

in, then. One thing I learned from the little hitch I served in the army is that the way to stay outa trouble is not to do anything an officer didn't tell you to."

His eyes widening, Henry looked at Longarm, and a frown slowly grew on his face. "Why, that sounds a bit selfish to me, Marshal Long. Goodness, if everybody took that kind of attitude and didn't volunteer to do things, nothing would ever get done!"

"Maybe not," Longarm replied. "But half the trouble folks get into today is when they do things they never ought to."

Although Longarm's tone was mild enough, the clerk apparently took his words as a rebuff, and stayed silent during the rest of the ride to the federal building. Henry's face was still pulled into a thoughtful frown when Longarm alighted from the hack and waved him on his way.

Never a beehive of activity, Denver's new federal building seemed completely deserted as Longarm climbed the stairs to the second floor. He entered the office without knocking. The door to Vail's private office stood ajar, and he could hear voices coming from the room. As he closed the hall door, Vail raised his voice.

"Come on in, Long," he called. "You certainly took your time getting here."

"Now, Billy, if I'd've known you intended to call me in to work on my day off, I'd've just come here from the depot last night and waited for you," Longarm said. He started across the outer office to Vail's private room. "All I hope is that whatever kinda case you're going to send me out on will hold still long enough for me to get a bite of breakfast before I leave."

"You'll have breakfast, all right," Vail promised. "But it'll be in the diner of the southbound Denver & Rio Grande train that pulls out in about an hour."

Longarm stepped into Vail's office while the chief marshal was speaking. He halted when he saw a man sitting in the red morocco-upholstered chair that he favored for himself. As Longarm stopped in the doorway, the stranger rose.

"Meet Gregory Blanchard," Vail said. "Greg and I are old army friends. When I heard his story last night, I told him I'd put a good man on the case he's asked me to look into."

As he reached for Blanchard's hand, Longarm sized him up in a single quick glance. Vail's friend was a stocky, broad-shouldered man, and the hand he extended was callused and muscular. His face was square, and tanned in the manner typical of men who worked outdoors and seldom took off their hats: a deep tan covered his jaws and cheeks and extended an inch or so above his broad eyebrows, while the skin of his forehead above the narrow line of tan was white to the roots of his thick black hair.

Blanchard was clean-shaven and his eyes were dark brown. His nose showed signs of having been broken, perhaps more than once. Lumps of muscle bulged at the point of his jaw. His lower lip was full, his upper lip a thin line, almost invisible when his mouth was closed. He was wearing a hip-length corduroy jacket over a green wool shirt, and tan gabardine trousers tucked into calf-high boots with high saddle-heels.

"Billy's been telling me you're the man that can help me, if anybody can, Marshal Long," the rancher said. "And even if I haven't got much to help you with, I'll sure do what I can to give you a hand while you're at my place."

"Well, thanks, Mr. Blanchard," Longarm replied. "Except I still ain't got any idea what kind of case it is you need me to look into." Turning back to the chief marshal, he went on, "If you don't mind me asking, where's this new case at and what am I supposed to do?"

"You'll be going to New Mexico Territory," Vail replied. "Greg has a spread over in the northern part, up above Las Vegas on the Rio Diablo."

"That's in Terry Higgins's district." Longarm frowned.

"Don't you think I know that?" Vail asked. "It was Higgins who sent Greg here to Denver. It seems all his deputy marshals are down in the southwest corner of New Mexico right now, and likely to be there for a while. Higgins suggested you'd be a good man to put on this case, seeing that you know the Territory about as well as his own men do."

"Sounds like it's something important, if you're sending me all that way," Longarm said.

"It might be," Vail told him. "But you're going to have to get your details of the case from Greg, here. He knows them a lot better than I do, and if we stay in the office and start gabbing about it, you two are likely to miss your train."

"Now, hold on, Billy!" Longarm protested. "I got to have time to go back out to my room and get my gear together. That clerk of yours didn't tell me I was going to have to leave right away, so all I got with me is what I'm standing up in."

"I can't fault you for that," Vail said. "We'll pick up a hack downstairs and swing by your room, then go on to the depot together. That'll give us time to talk."

"What about my travel orders and papers?" Longarm asked.

"I'll take care of them when you get back," Vail replied. He opened the center drawer of his desk and took out a leather drawstring pouch. During the years he had been working under Vail, Longarm had seen the chief marshal take that pouch out only twice before, and now he realized the importance Vail attached to the new case. The chief marshal spilled a handful of gold coins from the pouch onto the top of his desk and pushed five shiny new double eagles and ten eagles toward him.

"This ought to see you through," Vail said. "If you run short, send me a wire."

"I'll sure do that, Billy," Longarm said quickly. "Because I ain't got much of my own money left to tide me over till next payday."

"Greg will fix you up with a horse and saddle," Vail went on. "And you'll be staying at his place, so I don't imagine you'll find yourself in a tight spot."

Blanchard spoke for the first time since he and Longarm had been introduced. "Don't worry about a thing, Billy. Or you, either, Marshal Long. I feel like I'm responsible for having Billy send you over to the Territory to help us out. I'll see that you have everything you need."

When the three stepped out of the federal building it was easy to see that, as was always the case, the early Sunday morning snow had brought out every hired carriage that operated in the city. Vail whistled the first one that passed and the hackie wheeled over to the curb. Longarm gave him directions. When they arrived at his rooming house, he took the stairs up to his room two at a time, and made quick work of tossing into his saddlebags the items he knew he would need. Then he grabbed his Winchester from the corner where it leaned between two cases and hurried back downstairs.

"I guess I'm as ready as I'll ever be," he told the others. "Anything I forgot, Billy, I'll buy with Uncle Sam's money."

"That means I'll have to check your expenses closer than I usually do," the chief marshal said, with a smile that didn't match his threat. "But as long as you keep within reason, I don't suppose I'll argue much."

"I imagine we can fix you up with almost anything you're short of," Blanchard volunteered. "My spread's not as big as I hope it'll be some day, but we manage."

"Just exactly where is your place?" Longarm asked. "We been jumping around so fast that I ain't even found out yet just exactly where I'm heading."

"You've likely been in the northeastern part of New Mexico Territory, I'd imagine," Blanchard said.

"Oh, sure. More'n once. But I don't know that part as good as I do farther south, along the Santa Fe line."

"Well, the Box B straddles the Rio Diablo," the rancher said. "It's not much of a river, but it's big for that part of the country. Enough to take care of the little herd I run, anyhow."

"It's been a while since I was through there." Longarm frowned. "I can't recall no decent rivers besides the Canadian that run in that part of the Territory."

"It's not likely the Diablo's on many maps," Blanchard told him. "But it flows southeast into the Mora, then the Mora flows on east into the south fork of the Canadian."

"As I recall that country, all of it sorta slides off, downhill toward the southeast," Longarm said thoughtfully. "But it's been a while since I rode through there."

"You'll remember it when you see it again, I suppose," Vail put in. Before he could say anything more, the hackie reined in at the Denver & Rio Grande depot. Above the roof of the low-slung cut-stone building, they could see the smokestack of a locomotive puffing. Vail nodded toward the white plumes. "You two had better step lively. The engineer's getting up steam to pull out."

Blanchard swung out of the hack to the curb. "I've got my return ticket, so all we've got to do is get one for Marshal Long."

"I'll get mine from the conductor on the train," Longarm said, reaching for his rifle and saddlebags. "Billy, I guess you can look for me back when you see me."

Before Vail could answer, Longarm was gone, his long legs churning as the train whistle blew the two short toots signalling its departure. He made the coach steps behind Blanchard just as the train began moving, and followed the rancher down the

15

coach aisle. The train was far from being crowded; many people did not like to travel on Sunday.

Blanchard slid into the first pair of vacant seats and Longarm sat down beside him. The two men sat in silence while the locomotive picked up speed, watching Denver's spreading suburbs until houses gave way to broken country. When the last houses were behind them and nothing except the low-humped Rocky Mountain foothills showed through the window, the coach jumped and jerked a bit as the engineer opened the throttle still wider.

Judging that the time had come to find out what sort of case he was going on, Longarm turned to his companion. "You know, I still ain't got an idea in the world what this is all about. It'd settle my mind a lot if you'd tell me why you came looking for help from Billy when you got a sheriff or marshal a whole hell of a lot closer than either Santa Fe or Denver."

"I had an idea that was the first question you'd be asking me, Marshal Long. Now that we're not in any hurry, I'll give you the whole story."

"Before you start talking, there's one thing I'd like to say," Longarm told the rancher. "You're an old army buddy of Billy's, and you don't know me from Adam's off ox. But since we're gonna be working together a while, I got a sorta nickname—Longarm—that my friends call me."

"Well, my friends call me Greg," Blanchard said.

"Done," Longarm said. He fished one of his thin cheroots out of his vest pocket and lighted it. "Now, I'm right interested in hearing about whatever it is that's bothering you."

"Maybe I'd better tell you a little bit about my ranch first," Greg said. "It's a one-man spread now. I've got a son that's just about old enough to give me some real help. In a couple of years he'll turn sixteen; then I can start building up my herd. But right now, it's up to my wife and boy and me to keep the place going, and even if it's not really big, it sure means a lot of work for the three of us."

"A man's got to start someplace," Longarm observed as he puffed out a cloud of smoke. "And I'd say there's been a lot of big spreads started just the way you're doing."

"Sure," Greg nodded. "But my wife's sister is visiting us from back East right now, so that takes a little bit of strain off of Essie—my wife's name's Estelle, but we call her Essie—

16

and gives her somebody to talk to while Frank and I are out on the range working the cattle."

"Except there's something come up that's bothering you bad enough to look to the law for help," Longarm observed.

Blanchard nodded. "That's right, Longarm. Something real funny's happening upstream on the Rio Diablo."

"I take it you don't mean funny as in laughter—you mean odd."

Blanchard nodded. "Maybe it'll sound to you like I'm seeing ghosts under the bed. But somebody or something is killing cattle upstream from my place and letting their carcasses float down the river."

Longarm sat silent for a moment, a thoughtful frown growing on his face. Then he asked, "I guess you've hauled some of them carcasses to shore and looked at 'em?"

"Of course I have, at least a couple. Most of them are yearlings, and if any of them were shot or had their throats cut I'd've noticed it."

"Did you ever just let one go on floating downstream and ride alongside of it to see what happened to it?"

"Two or three times," Blanchard replied. "But every time I tried to follow one it got dark and I couldn't see the carcass any more, so I had to turn back."

"So you don't know whether the steers was killed or just keeled over and died, the way cattle do sometimes?"

"No. But my wife's sister—her name's Zenia—her husband was a veterinary doctor. She says those cattle died from anthrax, and she sure ought to know. And if you don't know it already, Longarm, if there's anything that scares the hell out of everybody who has anything to do with cattle, anthrax is it. I kept shaking in my boots till I couldn't stand it any longer. That's why I started out looking for help. If Zenia's right, everybody within a hundred miles of my ranch is just sitting on top of a volcano that might blow up at any minute and wipe all of us out!"

Chapter 3

Longarm stared at Greg for a moment, his jaw dropping, his cheroot motionless in his hand. At last he said, "Maybe you better tell me that again. I can't believe I heard you right."

"You heard me right," Blanchard told him. "I said anthrax, and that's just what I meant."

"Now tell me why you said it," Longarm suggested.

"Because most of those steers floating down the Rio Diablo looked like they died from some kind of cattle disease. When I saw the first one, I just figured it was a critter that had stepped off a steep bluff in that broken country northwest of my spread and broke its neck."

"How come you didn't drag it to shore and make sure?"

"Because the horse I was riding that day had gone lame and I was in a hurry to get home."

Longarm nodded, thinking that was about how he would have acted if he had been in Greg's place. He said, "But you seen more of them floating carcasses later on. It seems to me

18

you'd've been a mite curious about what killed 'em."

"I was, Longarm. When I saw another one a week or so later and two or three more during the next month, I realized there had to be something wrong."

"But you wasn't interested enough to find out?"

"Oh, I was interested, all right. But when I'd mentioned that first carcass, Zenia warned me that if I saw any more, I'd better not touch them unless I was wearing gutta-percha gloves. She said just touching any animal that died from anthrax could infect me."

"From what I've heard, she was right about that," Longarm nodded. "But I still can't figure out why you was so quick to figure what killed 'em if you didn't take a close look. Did you ever see an anthrax-sick steer?"

Greg shook his head. "No. It was actually Zenia who had the idea first. She's seen anthrax cases."

"Back East?"

"I guess Missouri's what folks call East, now. But that's where Essie and Zenia grew up."

"Farm family, I guess?"

"Yes. But it wasn't on the farm where Zenia learned about anthrax. She's only seen it in farm animals, of course. Her husband was a veterinary doctor. She said she hadn't seen many anthrax cases, but the steers I saw hadn't been butchered, so she decided they must've died from some sort of cattle sickness, and anthrax is the most common one."

"Well, I ain't in no position to say your sister-in-law's wrong, Greg, because as long as I been traipsing through cattle country, I ain't seen more'n about three cases of anthrax myself. But it sure seems like to me it'd be hard to tell just from looking at a dead steer that anthrax was what killed it."

"That's about what Zenia said," Greg nodded. "She told me that you've got to cut the critter up before you can be certain, and she said that if you're not real careful you can catch the anthrax just by touching its carcass."

"I've heard others say the same thing," Longarm agreed. "But there's still something I can't figure out about this. Why in tunket did you run to Billy Vail with your story?"

"I wouldn't call it running," Greg frowned. "Like I told you, I went to Santa Fe and tried to get the Territory's chief marshal to do something, and he's the one who suggested I try Billy."

"Don't you have a local sheriff or constable in that Rio Diablo country?"

"There's a constable in Watrous, but he doesn't have any authority outside the town limits. Las Vegas is the next nearest town to the ranch, but their policemen are in the same fix as the Watrous constable."

"Well, I guess you done the best you could, unless you'd thought to try the army. I ain't seen a post yet that don't have a veterinary doctor. How about Fort Union, up north of Las Vegas?"

Blanchard shook his head. "Fort Union's all but gone now, Longarm. The army's moved the staff officers back to what's left of Fort Marcy in Santa Fe and sent most of the troops down south to Apache country. Besides that, it's a good thirty miles from my place, and the old supply road's in such bad shape that I'd hate to try to get a wagon over it."

"I can see that'd leave you without much choice," Longarm said. "And I don't guess there's any other ranches close by you could look to for help or advice?"

"Well, I've heard that Colonel Goodnight's just bought a spread up to the north, along the Cimarron Cutoff, but he hasn't begun working it yet. With that little ranch of mine squeezed in between Goodnight on the north and the Maxwell Grant on the south, I feel like I'm out on a limb and somebody's sawing at it between me and the tree trunk."

"If there's not any more ranches close by, where's the dead cattle coming from?"

"Oh, there's a few homesteaders to the north of me," Greg frowned. "Most of them run kitchen herds, a dozen head or so."

"I don't know how I'm going to be able to do much of anything, Greg," Longarm said after a few moments of silent thought. "There just ain't much a man can sink his teeth into on this case. It'd seem to me it's a job for the Army's Sanitary Corps. Have you thought about asking them for some help?"

"That was the first thing Zenia thought of when I began seeing those dead steers so regularly," Greg replied. "You see, her husband was with the Sanitary Corps before they got married. He went down into Mexico when that big *aftosa* scare came up to help them try to close the border to diseased critters."

"*Aftosa*'s bad enough," Longarm said, shaking his head. "I

had a little run-in a while back with a gang that was setting out to smuggle some hoof-and-mouth infected stock across the border, so I know what it's like."

"At least hoof-and-mouth only hits cattle," Greg said. "But anthrax can wipe out all kinds of animals and kill people, too."

"So they say," Longarm nodded. Glancing out the window, he saw that the train had entered the first level stretch that lay between Denver and Colorado Springs. He felt a yawn coming on and tried unsuccessfully to suppress it. "I guess you got a good night's sleep, Greg, which is more than I can say I did. If you don't mind, I'm just going to lean back and doze a few minutes. We got plenty of time to do our talking later on."

In spite of Longarm's constant prodding, he learned little more about the situation on Blanchard's ranch during the hours that followed. While Greg was not reticent in discussing his family or the difficulties of getting a small spread started in the isolation of northern New Mexico Territory, he had little to add to what he had already revealed about the suspected anthrax infestation.

By the time Pike's Peak fell behind them, Longarm had decided he was likely to learn little more. He and Blanchard chatted idly while the train rolled smoothly along on the generally level terrain between the last mountain outcrops and the saucer-like alluvial plain to the east.

In mid-afternoon, when the conductor walked through the coaches calling the Trinidad stop, Longarm turned to his companion and said, "I don't know how you feel, Greg, but for the last half-hour my belly's been asking me who cut my throat."

"I feel pretty much like you do, I guess," the rancher replied. "Those butcher-boy sandwiches we had at noon didn't do much for me."

"Well, I know where there's one pretty fair restaurant in Trinidad," Longarm told him. "And we'll have almost an hour between trains, time for us to stoke up."

"I'll take your word for wherever we go, Longarm. I didn't have time on the trip up to Denver to do more than go from the UP depot to the D&RG."

"Oh, Trinidad's a right nice little town. Besides the restaurant, I been in a few of the saloons there and seen one or two that's got a real good free lunch."

"I don't drink myself, but if you'd rather go to a saloon,

I'll tag along and have a bottle of sarsaparilla or something," Blanchard offered. "I guess sarsaparilla would give me the right to eat a bite of their free lunch."

"Don't worry about that. Unless there's a saloon in whatever town we'll stop at to get to your ranch, I aim to buy me a bottle of Tom Moore to take along."

"There's no restaurant in Valmora, where we'll have to get off, because I left my horse in the livery stable there," Blanchard said. "So we'd better eat enough in Trinidad to tide us over until we get to the ranch tonight. The closest thing Valmora's got to a restaurant is a *cantina* that serves a pretty good beer, but no food."

"We'll make it Trinidad, then," Longarm said. Almost before he had finished speaking, the wailing toots of the engineer whistling the station drifted back to the coach. The first houses on the outskirts of Trinidad began to flash past the windows as the train began slowing for its stop. The town held memories for Longarm, and he glanced out the window, remembering the picnic he had had with Christina Albee on a bluff overlooking the town.

That had been a while back, and spurred by the demands for coal from its mines by the D&RG and the Santa Fe, Trinidad had grown quite a bit. It was still a compact town, but from the high railroad grade that overlooked the community Longarm could see that its main street was much longer.

There were more brick buildings lining the downtown streets than on his last visit, and on two sides of the business section the houses of native adobe were now outnumbered by residences of dark red brick spaced in the neat geometric squares of planned city blocks. Adobe dwellings still covered most of the shallow valley beyond the town's core, and these were scattered in the helter-skelter fashion that earlier had characterized the entire settlement. The mines had grown both in size and number, and hoists were visible in several places now.

Longarm had been so interested in his observation of the bluffs that rose above Trinidad, trying to locate the wide ledge where he and Tina had picnicked, that he was only half aware that the train had stopped. Greg said, "We'd better get off, if we expect to find a place where we can eat supper."

Picking up his saddlebags and rifle, Longarm tossed the bags over one shoulder and held the Winchester in the crook of his elbow as he followed Blanchard to the coach door.

Though the sky was clear and the sun bright, the brisk breeze that swept across the station platform carried a breath of coolness from the snowbanks that still stood on the mountain peaks surrounding the town. The two men stepped off the platform and started down the street.

Longarm said, "The place we're looking for is the Imperial Saloon. It's on the main street just a little ways toward where all the stores are crowded up."

Behind them they heard the clatter of hoofbeats on the hard-baked surface of the road. Both men automatically stepped a bit closer to the edge of the road to give the approaching riders plenty of room to pass. Longarm slid a cigar from his pocket and was holding a match to it as the three horsemen passed. He puffed the cheroot's end to an even glow and lifted his eyes from its tip just as one of the men who had ridden by turned to glance back.

When he saw the rider's face, Longarm stopped dead in his tracks. The riders did not pause, and the man who had turned his head was no longer looking at Longarm and Blanchard, but was speaking to one of his companions. Blanchard came to a halt when Longarm stopped, a puzzled frown puckering his eyebrows.

"Why're you stopping, Longarm?" Greg asked. "You said that saloon we're looking for is—"

"It is. But we ain't going there for a minute. Here." He handed Blanchard his saddlebags. "Take these along with you and hang on to them. Now get moving toward that building over there, and keep outa the way."

"What's the matter?"

"That fellow on the horse in the middle is Lefty Coelo. He oughta be in the state pen at Canon City, because he's got a date with the hangman two weeks from now."

"Are you sure about that?"

"Damned sure. I arrested him myself after he killed a Wells Fargo driver when he tried to stop Coelo from robbing his wagon that was carrying a shipment of money from the Denver Mint."

"What about the other two?"

"I didn't get a look at their faces, but if they're with Coelo they'll be outlaws, too."

"But there are three of them—" Greg began.

Longarm cut him short. "That don't make no never-mind.

23

Now, do like I told you, Greg. Get outa the way, because it's likely Coelo and his two friends will put up a fight."

Without waiting to see whether Blanchard had followed his instructions, Longarm started running after the three riders. They were twenty yards ahead of him, silhouetted against the declining sun, but as wanted men had a habit of doing, one of them looked back over his shoulder.

Shouting a warning to his companions, the outlaw brought his hand back to draw the revolver that dangled from his hip holster. Longarm did not wait for the outlaw's gun to clear leather. He snapshotted and the man's body jerked as the Winchester's slug found its mark.

Sagging, the outlaw started toppling slowly from his horse. Panicked by the unfamiliar shifting of its falling rider, the animal reared and bolted, its hooves kicking up spurts of gravel from the street.

Longarm shifted his aim to Coelo, who had been riding next to the man who had now fallen from his saddle, but the cracking report of the Winchester had alerted both the others. Coelo and his remaining companion had their revolvers out by now, and while they were drawing they spurred their mounts into a run. As they galloped away, they twisted in their saddles to fire at Longarm.

He had started running toward the pair as soon as he'd gotten off his first shot. The slugs from the outlaws' pistols whistled past him, but Longarm did not stop. He shot from the hip on the run, handling the Winchester as though it was a pistol, bringing its barrel almost vertically upright after each shot to pump a fresh shell into the chamber.

It wasn't the kind of shooting Longarm liked to do, for it sacrificed accuracy in favor of quick firing, but the two outlaws both carried rifles in their saddle scabbards and Longarm knew that he had to even the odds against him before they emptied their revolvers and reached for the longer-range, more accurate weapons.

A pistol slug raising dust at his feet brought Longarm to a halt. He stopped long enough to get off another hastily aimed shot. The horse ridden by one of the desperadoes reared, neighed shrilly, then staggered and went down. Somehow the rider managed to free his booted feet from the stirrups, for he rolled off the horse as the animal collapsed to the dirt, then dropped behind the shelter of its carcass.

Longarm dropped to the ground himself when a slug from the outlaw who was still mounted passed within an inch of his ear. The fugitive who had sheltered behind the fallen horse was reaching across the animal with one arm, struggling to get his rifle out of his scabbard, but the weight of the dead animal rested on the weapon.

Longarm took quick aim at the slender target and let off a shot. The lead thudded into the dead animal's back an inch from the outlaw's arm, and he drew it back quickly to safety. In a moment, he raised his head quickly, swivelled his revolver, and fired in Longarm's general direction, but the slug whistled harmlessly high.

By now Longarm was close enough to recognize the only one of the outlaw trio still mounted. It was Coelo, the condemned killer, who had obviously escaped from the Canon City pen. He fired at Longarm, the slug plowing into the dirt within inches of the lawman's feet. Coelo wheeled his mount and returned to help his companion. The outlaw's body was shielded by the neck and head of his horse as he leaned down. Longarm swung his rifle around and waited until Coelo raised up, bringing the unhorsed thug with him, twisting in his saddle to help his companion onto his own mount's crupper.

As the second outlaw swung twisting in mid-air he glimpsed Longarm levelling his rifle and raised the revolver which was still grasped in his hand. Longarm saw the pistol coming up and knew that he had small chance of hitting the man's arm. Shifting his aim, he let off a shot at the man in the saddle. The slug sailed past the riders. Both men dropped to the ground and lay prone, offering no sure target.

Riderless now, Coelo's mount galloped off as the pair scuttled like crabs to reach the protection of the dead horse's carcass. Longarm also dropped flat. He was too old a hand to offer himself as a standing target. One of the fugitives raised his revolver above the animal's belly and sent an unaimed shot whistling harmlessly above Longarm's head, then quickly dropped his gun hand.

In the sudden hush that followed the sustained shooting, Longarm could hear voices, shouts, and words too faint to be intelligible coming from streets beyond the barricaded outlaws.

"Coelo!" Longarm called loudly. "You and your friend might as well get up! There's men coming up behind you, and most of 'em will be carrying guns!"

"And they'll be as likely to shoot at you as they will at us!" the barricaded outlaw shouted back.

Longarm recognized the truth of the fugitive's statement. He knew he had to end the standoff quickly. Scuttling like a crab, his belly hugging the ground, he began crawling toward the men sheltered behind the fallen horse. He left his rifle behind him and drew his Colt as he edged ahead.

Chapter 4

As Longarm advanced toward the two outlaws sheltered behind the dead horse, he made no effort to move silently. The noise of the approaching crowd would cover the scraping of his boots on the hard-baked soil.

He moved with his gun hand ahead of him, his finger on the Colt's trigger. He could hear no sounds coming from the barricaded pair. It seemed as though hours had passed since he had started crawling, but at last he was within arm's length of the dead animal.

Longarm stopped, debating whether to attack head-on or to circle the carcass and catch the fugitives off-guard. He had lain motionless only a few seconds when he saw the muzzle of a revolver slide slowly into view above the horse's flank. Longarm froze, his eyes glued to the worn blued steel cylinder.

The muzzle of the threatening weapon remained motionless while a dozen seconds ticked off. Then the revolver muzzle twitched almost imperceptibly and Longarm adjusted the aim of his own pistol a hairsbreadth. His point of aim was now a bit to the right and an inch above the muzzle of the hidden gunman's weapon.

Suddenly Coelo's head popped up over the curved flank of the horse. Longarm triggered off his shot. At almost point-blank range, the heavy slug from the colt crashed into the bridge of the outlaw's nose, plowed through his skull, and sent a spattering spurt of blood and brain tissue out the back of his head.

The revolver in the dead man's hand slid out of sight and fell with a clatter onto the stone-strewn ground behind the horse.

When the remaining outlaw did not show himself, Longarm began circling the horse's carcass. He rounded its head just as the first men in the approaching crowd reached the scene. A glance was enough to show him that one of the random shots he had let off while the third man was dangling in mid-air had found its mark. The third outlaw was as dead as the other two.

Standing up, Longarm holstered his Colt and started back to get his rifle. He had taken only two or three steps when a shot rang out behind him and hot lead whistled above his head. At the same time a man's voice called from the crowd, "Stop right in your tracks, mister, or you won't make any more!"

Longarm recognized the voice of authority, though he did not know who had spoken. He halted at once and spread his arms away from his sides. The men who had been drawn to the scene by the gunfire stopped short of the bodies and stood gazing and staring, talking in whispers.

"That's fine," said the man who had commanded him to stop. "Now just stay the way you are till I can get a look at you. I got my pistol in my hand. It's cocked and ready, and it's got a hair trigger, so don't make no mistake about me being serious."

"You don't need to worry," Longarm called without turning his head. "I take it you're a lawman, and I'm one myself. Come on up and we'll talk."

Footsteps grated on the gravel behind him, and Longarm felt a hand lift his Colt from its holster. Then the man stepped around in front of him.

"Oh, hell!" he said. "I know who you are, even if we never have bumped into each other before. You're the federal marshal named Long, the one folks call Longarm."

"That's right," Longarm said. "I take it you're the law officer in charge here?"

The other man nodded, holstering his pistol and handing Longarm the Colt. "Name's Godell. Deputy sheriff and acting town marshal. I sure hope you're not mad because I called you the way I did."

Godell extended his hand and the two men shook. As Longarm holstered his Colt, he said, "I ain't a bit upset, Godell. I figure I'd've done just what you did if I'd come up on a shootout where three men was stretched out dead and another one was walking away from 'em."

Looking at the bodies sprawled on the ground, Godell nodded. "Now I know who you are, I don't need much explanation, Marshal Long. Them bodies sorta speak for themselves." He turned back to the crowd and raised his voice. "The shooting's all over, so you men can go back about your business. Snaky, you go tell Pat he's got some bodies to take care of. The rest of you suit yourselves about staying, because when Pat gets here he'll need a hand loading the dead men into his wagon."

For a moment the onlookers did not move. Then they began slowly drifting away. Godell turned back to Longarm. "I don't guess you'd mind telling me who these fellows are, and what set off the shooting?"

"Not a bit, except that I don't know but one of 'em. He's Lefty Coelo, and some way he managed to escape from the death cell at the Canon City pen."

"I don't guess I need to ask you if you're sure about him being who you say he is."

"Oh, I'm sure, all right. I know him a mite better'n I know you right now, because I delivered him there myself. I really didn't get a good look at the other two, but from the glimpses I got of their faces, both of 'em are strangers to me."

"Let's have a look," Godell suggested. Longarm followed him around the carcass of the horse to where Coelo and his companions lay sprawled. Godell went on, "Sure. I know both of 'em. That one's Sam Prosner; the other one's Jake Rails."

"Are they just locals, or do they ride the owlhoot trail?"

"Well, I see them in town a couple of times a month." The Trinidad officer frowned. "They don't work anywhere regular, but they've always got plenty of money."

"Except you don't know where it comes from?"

"That's about the size of it," Godell said. "As far as I know, they aren't on anybody's Wanted list right now."

"They wouldn't've cut down on me if they hadn't been with Lefty Coelo, I imagine," Longarm said. "It was Lefty who drew first. The minute he saw me he knew he'd got to the end of his string. After he pulled his gun, these others didn't have much choice except to do the same. They'd have to know Lefty had broke out of the pen somehow, and that I recognized him right off."

"That's something else you can be sure about, Longarm. For what it's worth to you, I've had Prosser and Rails on my list for a long time. My hunch is they ride with the Antrim gang when there's a big job on, but I've never been able to prove it."

"Looks like they've just proved it for you," Longarm said. He frowned and went on thoughtfully, "Antrim. I know that name from over in the Texas Panhandle. There's a young cowboy turned outlaw there that calls himself Billy the Kid, but his real name's Antrim, from what I understand."

"He'd be from the same family that Joe Antrim is," Godell said. "Their daddy's a blacksmith that used to work around here till he moved on. South, someplace down close to the Mexican border. Neither one of his boys went along, though. Joe stayed here, and he's still in the neighborhood someplace, likely closer to Raton than here. He keeps getting in and out of trouble, but I'd sorta lost track of Billy until you said he's over in the Texas Panhandle."

"Family really gets around, don't it?" Longarm commented.

"So it seems. At least, Joe does, but he's smart enough not to get out of line around here. I keep pretty close tabs on him, and right now he's not wanted for anything."

"You don't suppose these three was on their way to join him, do you?" Longarm asked. "It'd make sense to me if Coelo was trying to get over the border into New Mexico Territory before the word spread that he'd broke outa the pen."

"It's as good a guess as any, I suppose," Godell agreed. "But it's not likely we'll ever know. These three sure won't be telling us anything."

Longarm nodded, then gestured to the three bodies. "By rights, I'm responsible for seeing that these bodies get buried, but I hope you won't mind taking care of that for me. If you have to hire somebody to dig their graves and cover 'em, send the bill to my chief in Denver. I'll see it's taken care of."

"Now that's not necessary, Longarm. I've got three or four hoboes in jail here, working off vagrancy fines. I'll put the money they get grave-digging against what they owe, and they'll get out a day or so earlier, so I'll save on my food bill."

"I'm mighty obliged for your help," Longarm told him. "I'm in a hurry, just starting on a case. Me and the fellow I'm travelling with need to eat before we catch the southbound Santa Fe passenger train."

"You go on about your business, Marshal Long," Godell said. "I'll see everything's all tied up neat. And any time you find yourself in Trinidad with some extra time on your hands, be sure to drop in at the office for a visit."

"Thanks. I'll do that," Longarm said.

Realizing that in the flurry of the gunfight he had forgotten about Greg Blanchard, Longarm looked around as Godell moved away to encourage what was left of the crowd to scatter. Seeing the rancher standing off to one side, Longarm started toward him.

"You sure made quick work of those three," Blanchard said.

"When you get into a shooting scrape, Greg, the sooner you end it, the better. Now, let's see if we can find some grub and pick me up a bottle of Tom Moore. I'd like a tot before we eat, and I imagine you could use one, too, even if you don't usually drink much."

"I guess I could, at that. It's not every day of the week that I watch a man I know get into a gunfight. I feel a little bit funny about not jumping in to help you, but I don't even carry a gun, except for a rifle when I'm riding range."

"There's not much reason why you should," Longarm told him.

"I can see why you'd have to, though," Blanchard went on. "Do you run into things like this very often?"

"Often enough to keep me awake," Longarm said. He pointed to the swinging doors of a saloon on the street ahead. "If I recall rightly, that's the place we're looking for."

For Longarm, the rest of the trip was a retracing of earlier journeys that had taken him across the rolling grasslands of the Rocky Mountain foothills and the eastern slopes of the Sangre de Cristo Mountains. A few miles south of Trinidad the train

31

crossed the border between Colorado and New Mexico Territory, but the character of the land changed very little. There was no real dividing line where one range stopped and the other began, though the peaks of the Sangre de Cristos were much less imposing than those of the Rockies.

Below the brown rock crests that marked the snowline, the mountainsides were dark green with firs and cedars which grew in a wide belt between the bare peaks and the brighter green of the grasses that covered the lower slopes. It was not smooth, level prairie, but rolling land, with wide, shallow valleys spreading between broad, rounded ridges.

There were few trees and fewer streams, and the streams were gently flowing brooks, not rushing rivers. After the tracks crossed the Vermijo River just above the point where it flowed into the Canadian, there were even fewer streams to be seen. The tracks began the gentle curve that would take them in an arc around the flanks of the Sangre de Cristo Mountains.

"How in tunket do you get enough water for your stock?" Longarm asked Greg as the train rumbled over the trestle spanning a small stream. "This is the first creek I've seen in twenty miles that a tall man couldn't step across."

"Oh, we manage with what comes down the Rio Diablo and a few springs I've turned into water holes," the rancher replied. "Essie and I moved out here about seven years ago, and so far we've only had one really dry summer to worry about."

"You run a pretty good-sized herd, do you?"

"Not by Texas or Colorado standards," Blanchard said with a smile. "To tell you the truth, I had my eye on the land just north of my place, but before I could get up the money to buy it, Colonel Goodnight beat me to it. Of course, he's got all the money in the world, compared to what I've got."

"I didn't see much cattle on the range, if what we've been crossing is Goodnight land."

"It is," the rancher told him. "But the colonel hasn't moved any stock onto it yet. I heard the real reason he bought the land up here was to be sure nobody'd try to close off the Cimarron Cutoff that he scouted for their market herds during the big trail-drive days."

"Well, like you said, the colonel's got plenty of money to buy whatever he takes a fancy to," Longarm said. "How much farther is it to your spread, Greg?"

"About another half-hour from where we are right now. It doesn't run all the way to the railroad, but I guess you noticed that there aren't any fences to keep me from driving my little herd to market."

"How many head do you move in a season?"

"Nowhere near as many as I'd like to," Greg said, shaking his head. "Just a few hundred. And when I ship out I only have to push them to Watrous. It's only a few miles south of Valmora. The Santa Fe's got pens and loading chutes there, and since the last time I loaded a shipment I heard they're putting in a big new roundhouse there, too."

"It's a bigger place than Valmora, then?"

"Not by very much. Just another whistle stop, but it's almost the same distance from the ranch as Valmora."

"You know, it's a funny thing," Longarm remarked. "I guess I've rode the Santa Fe south from Denver maybe a dozen times, and I never have noticed those two stations."

"Probably because they're not real stations," the rancher suggested. "I'd bet not more than one Santa Fe train out of ten stops at either place."

Longarm was silent for a moment while he lighted a cheroot. Then he said, "Greg, let's get back to what we was talking about before we stopped at Trinidad and got sidetracked by those outlaws."

"Anthrax?"

"That, and the steer carcasses you've seen floating down the Rio Diablo."

"What about them, Longarm? I've told you about all there is to tell."

"How come you never did ride all the way alongside the river and find out where the floating carcasses end up?"

"Hell, I know where they wind up! The Rio Diablo flows into the Mora, and the Mora empties into the Canadian. If you've ever been around the Canadian, you'll remember that it winds around about a third of Texas before it joins the Red."

"And you figure the dead critters go all the way?"

"I hadn't given it that much thought, because once they're off my land, I don't really care. But now that you've brought it up, my guess is that when the gas that's bloated up those dead steers leaks away, they sink and roll along the bottom until they hit a stretch of quicksand."

Longarm nodded thoughtfully and said, "I expect that might be where they go, at that. I know a little bit about them sinkholes in the Canadian."

Greg went on, "The fact is that I've got my hands full taking care of the steers that're on the hoof. I don't have time to waste tracking down dead ones."

"Well, I just might put in a little time doing that, soon as I know the lay of the land," Longarm remarked. The locomotive whistle shrieked and the train began to slacken speed.

"We're coming into Valmora," Blanchard said. He glanced out the window. The sun was slanting down in the west now, only a small strip of blue sky showing between its bottom rim and the ragged crests of the Sangre de Cristos. "If we don't waste too much time here, we'll be able to get to the ranch house before full dark."

"It don't look to me like there's much here to waste time on," Longarm commented as he peered out the coach window.

"There's not," Greg agreed, "but it's the only town we've got close by, except Watrous." He stood up as the train stopped and went on, "We'd better get a move on, Longarm. They don't keep this train standing here any longer than it takes for us to get off it, and if the engineer gets impatient he's liable to start before we're even out of the coach."

Longarm grabbed his rifle and saddlebags and followed the rancher to the coach door. Greg hit the ground first, a long step, since the conductor hadn't bothered to provide the usual stepstool. As Longarm swung off the coach, the engineer tooted the whistle and the train began to move. It pulled away, leaving Longarm and Greg standing alone beside the track. Longarm swivelled his head from side to side, surveying the town.

Valmora was one of those small settlements Longarm had learned were commonplace in the New Mexico's northern mountains. There seemed to be no real reason for its existence. The town was not so much a town as a straggled clump of widely spaced individual dwellings. It had no orderly pattern of streets. The small houses of which it was composed stood at odd angles to one another, their slabstone walls rising from barren soil that, judging from the sparse grasses and lack of weeds, must have been almost infertile.

Whether from lack of water or the unsuitability of the soil, adobe houses were rare. Of the thirty or forty scattered structures that stretched away from the railroad tracks, only half a dozen were built of adobe bricks and had the flat-topped roofs which were almost standard elsewhere in New Mexico Territory.

In Valmora, thin slabs of the porous sandstone that shelved out in layers from the light tan soil were the most common building material. There was a plentiful supply of the stone and it was available for the taking. It was soft and easy to break into rectangular slabs which could be laid in overlapping tiers like thin bricks, and held in place with mud to form low walls.

Most of the houses were roofed with overlapped tin sheets nailed to rafters that were slanted front to back. Holes left for doors and windows had to be framed in with expensive, hard-to-obtain lumber, so in all but a handful of the scattered houses the windows were small and the doors low and narrow. The stone used in their walls ranged in color from deep reddish-brown to pale milky cream, and those who had built the houses had paid no attention to color compatibility when erecting the house walls, which gave them a piebald look.

Beside the railroad track there was a one-room depot which also served as a baggage shed and housed the stationmaster. It was one of two carpenter-built structures in the hamlet, and looked out of place with its neat board walls painted in the road's standard yellowish tan and brown. The other lumber building was the store, which was also the livery stable. The sheds that stood behind it were of native stone.

"There's no use wasting time," Greg said, indicating the declining sun with a nod. "Let's go over to the livery and see about getting you a horse. Now that I'm almost home, I'm anxious to get back to the ranch."

Chapter 5

"You'll be able to see the house as soon as we get over this next hump," Greg told Longarm as they rode toward the crest of a grassy ridge, their elongating shadows darkening the ground ahead of them.

Blanchard and Longarm had been riding steadily for a bit over an hour since leaving Valmora. Greg's horse was rested after having stood idle in the livery stable for several days, and Longarm's rented gelding was equally fresh. Except for a few low rounded ridges that curved across their route, the ground sloped to the east in a gentle fall which made the going easy on their mounts. The terrain was generally treeless, the tallest growth an occasional stunted *piñon*, more brush than tree at this low altitude. It was not prairie but grassland, the narrow waving tips of the tall growth swaying in a gentle breeze.

"I'll tell you this, Greg," Longarm replied. "Not that it's anything you don't know already, but you sure got some mighty pretty rangeland here. Can't say I blame you for wanting to settle down in this place."

"Well, I don't ever expect to get rich off a spread this size, but by the time I got out here to the West it was too late to pick up big hunks of land. I'm not complaining, though. My spread's about the right size for me to handle by myself."

"You don't ever hire any hands, then?"

"Oh, sometimes when a drifter stops by I'll put him to work for a week or two. There's always some jobs I don't have time to get around to doing. And my boy helps, of course."

They reached the top of the rise and the land fell away in a long downslope that stretched for three or four miles. A scant half-mile ahead the slope shelved to form a roughly flat expanse that was large enough to accommodate a small house, a moderate-sized corral, and a large barn. Like the house, the barn faced east. A spring wagon stood at one side of it.

There were three horses and a pair of mules in the corral. A ragged arc of young cottonwood trees grew north of the house and barn at the edge of the level area. A privy stood beyond the trees, almost hidden by their trunks. A short distance from the outhouse a huge pile of bare-limbed *piñon* trees stood in a heap.

Between the trees and the house were the tidy rows of a small garden. Far in the distance, cattle grazed on grass that came almost up to their bellies. A few strays wandered alone, distant from the herd.

"We're home," Greg said, waving toward the house. "And I don't mind telling you, I'm glad to be back."

"Looks like a nice place," Longarm told him.

"It is," Greg agreed. "Of course, it's not finished, and I don't guess it ever will be. Essie keeps telling me we need another room, but I've been too busy to add one."

"You'll get around to it sooner or later, I reckon," Longarm said.

In comparison with the size of the barn, the ranch house did look small. It was a ground-hugging rectangular board-and-batten structure. Such houses required a minimum of scarce and costly lumber, and even a novice at carpentry could quickly learn the skills required in using this type of construction.

From the appearance of the house, Longarm guessed that its interior had been partitioned into rooms in accordance with the almost universal frontier plan. Such houses were generally divided into three rooms: one big room stretching across the front that served as living room, dining room, and kitchen, and provided accommodations for guests, and two small bedrooms across the back, used by the family members.

"I've been thinking about the best place for you to sleep while you're here," Greg told Longarm as they drew closer to the house. "We put Essie's sister in my boy's room and he's sleeping in the front room. It's twice as big as the other two, and there's plenty of room for both you and Frank. Or, if you'd rather, you can sleep in the barn loft. There's plenty of hay in it, and you'll be about as comfortable there as you would in the house."

"It don't make all that much difference where I sleep, Greg," Longarm said. "But maybe the loft might be better. Your wife might just as soon not have me underfoot in her kitchen. And I can get a good night's sleep just about anyplace."

"We'll leave it at that, then," Blanchard nodded.

They rode on a short distance in silence, then Longarm said, "Let's see if I got my p's and q's straight about the way the land lays." He pointed to the right of the house. "This Rio Diablo you was talking about, I'd guess it's over that way?"

"You'd be guessing right. About three miles."

"And where does it come from?"

"It heads up in a big underground spring halfway up Agua Fria Mountain," Greg said, twisting in his saddle to point to one of the tallest of the peaks that towered behind them to the northwest. "I guess it must pick up some more water from other springs along the way, because it keeps up a pretty steady flow all summer. Then it winds around a lot through my range and empties into the Canadian."

"And you ain't seen any steers in the other rivers?"

Blanchard shook his head. "No. But I haven't watched any of them close, either. For all I know, there might be some floating down the Vermijo or the Quincho or the Altamira. All of them run full enough until snowmelt to float a carcass."

"All the other creeks empty into the Canadian, do they?"

"Sure. But the Vermijo and the Altamira don't feed the Rio Diablo."

"It looks to me like my first job's going to be following the rivers up to where they start," Longarm said. "If there's a place where somebody has been slaughtering steers along the bank, there's bound to be some sign of it left."

"Well, I'll give you what help I can," Greg promised. "But

it'll have to be after I catch up on the chores I didn't get finished before I took off for Denver."

"Oh, I can do a lot of noseying around on my own, Greg," Longarm said. 'You just figure on going about your regular business. When I run into something I need help on—"

He broke off as a shout sounded from the house. Both men looked ahead. A youth had come outside and seen them. He was followed by two women, who joined him in waving to the riders.

"Count on Frank to see me first," Greg smiled. "And that's Essie standing by him. Her sister Zenia's the one in back."

"Nice-looking family," Longarm said.

"They are, at that," Greg agreed. "I guess I'm a lucky man."

He toed his horse and pulled a few yards ahead of Longarm. Frank had grabbed his mother's hand and was pulling her along with him toward the approaching riders. Greg reined in and while he and Essie and Frank were standing in a three-way embrace, Longarm reached them and swung out of his saddle. He stood a few feet away until the trio had gone through the first greetings. Then Greg got one arm around his wife's waist and his other arm around Frank's shoulders and turned them to face Longarm. In the meantime, Zenia had moved closer to the group.

"My wife and boy, Longarm," Blanchard said. "Essie, this is Deputy United States Marshal Custis Long. Billy Vail sent him back here with me to see what he can find out about those dead steers we've been wondering about."

"A real United States marshal!" Frank exclaimed before anyone else could speak. "Do you have gunfights with bad men, and all stuff like that there?"

"Hush, Billy!" Essie reproved gently. "You'll have plenty of time to ask Marshal Long questions." Turning back to Longarm, she extended her hand. "You're surely welcome, Marshal Long. Those steer carcasses have been worrying us quite a while."

"I'm right pleased to meet you, Mrs. Blanchard." Longarm doffed his hat. "Greg's been bragging you up all the way here from Denver." Releasing Essie's hand, he held out his own to Frank and went on, "I do just about what any other man wearing a badge does, son, but it ain't all shooting and gunfights. But we'll talk about that later on."

Essie broke in to say, "Marshal Long, this is my sister, Zenia Harmon. I'm sure Greg mentioned her, too."

"He did," Longarm replied, taking the hand Zenia extended. Her grip was firm and her brief handshake positive.

"I'm pleased to meet you, Marshal Long," Zenia said. "But I don't see what good you can do here. A sanitary engineer is what we really need."

"Maybe I'm just here to do what I can because there's a lot more marshals than sanitary engineers in this part of the country," Longarm suggested.

"Well, whatever I can do to help, count on me, Marshal," she said. "I learned a little bit about animal diseases from my late husband, you know. I suppose Greg's told you he was a veterinary surgeon?"

"He did mention it, ma'am," Longarm replied. "I'm sure I'll need to ask you to give me a hand."

"Suppose you lead our horses down to the barn, Frank," Greg told his son. "Longarm and I need to wash the travel dirt off and then sit down and have a cup of that coffee I'm sure your mother's got on the stove."

As Frank led the horses away and the adults started toward the house, Longarm took stock of the women he'd just met. Essie Blanchard was quite a bit younger than her husband. She was a small woman, looking almost frail in her long, loose calico dress. There was nothing unusual about her features. They were pleasantly regular but not strongly defined, making her attractive enough without being beautiful, but she was pretty in a housewifely sort of way.

Zenia Harmon was a more mature edition of Essie. She was taller, and even wearing the loose calico dress that concealed her body's contours, it was easy to see that she was built more sturdily than her sister. Her facial features were also more strongly defined. Her nose was just a bit too large for beauty, and her strong jawline was oddly at variance with the lush fullness of her lips. Like Essie, she had dark blond hair and light blue eyes.

"I hope you and Greg had a pleasant trip from Denver, Marshal Long," Zenia said as they walked around the side of the house toward the front door.

"It was fine, except we had a little dust-up while we were changing trains in Trinidad," Longarm replied.

"By dust-up I suppose you mean trouble?"

"You'd have to call it that, I guess," he agreed. "But it didn't last but a few minutes, and it saved a lot of innocent folks around there from bigger trouble later on."

"Somehow I get the idea that you lead a rather troublesome life, Marshal."

"No more than most, Mrs. Harmon. Besides, I'm used to it."

"Tell me something, Marshal Long. What do you expect to do here?"

"Well, now, that's a question I can't answer yet. Not till I find out what's been going on."

"Surely Greg's told you?" she went on.

"Oh, sure, but it don't seem like he knows too much about what's happening himself."

"Marshal Long—"

"Excuse me for interrupting, ma'am," he broke in. "But I got a sorta nickname that I answer to better'n I do 'marshal.' If you could see your way clear to calling me by it, I'd be right obliged."

"Of course. What is it?"

"Longarm, ma'am."

She smiled. "I'll be glad to oblige you, Longarm. And, to be fair about it, you'll have to call me Zenia."

"Sure. It's a lot more friendly when folks that're going to be around together for quite a spell ain't so stiff and formal."

"You still haven't answered my question," she reminded him.

"Well, if you don't object, I'd like to put that off till I got a little bit more to go on with."

"That's fair enough," Zenia agreed. "Just so you don't forget that I'm waiting for an answer."

"Oh, I won't forget, Zenia," Longarm promised. "Soon as I can figure things out, I'll tell you."

They reached the front door as Longarm spoke, and he stood aside to let Zenia enter first. Essie Blanchard was at the big cast-iron kitchen range, stirring the coals of a dying fire. A big coffeepot stood on the top of the stove and cups had been put on the oilcloth cover of the table that stood a step or two away from it.

Greg had already settled down into a platform rocker. His hat lay on the floor beside him and he was leaning back, rocking gently, a contented smile on his face. He indicated a nearby

41

chair with a flick of his hand. Longarm sat down and followed his host's example by depositing his hat on the floor.

"Nothing like getting home, Longarm," Greg commented.

"Not when you got a family, I guess," Longarm agreed.

"You're not married, then, Marshal Long?" Essie asked.

"No, ma'am. I've seen too many men in my line of work have family troubles because their jobs keep 'em out at all hours, and because their wives worry too much about what might be happening to their husbands when they don't get home on time night after night because of some case they're on."

Frank came in carrying Longarm's rifle. He said, "When I was unsaddling the horses, I thought I'd better bring your gun in, Marshal Long, instead of just letting it lay in the barn."

"Why, thank you, Frank," Longarm said. "That reminds me, I got to clean it and my Colt, too, after that dust-up we run into at Trinidad."

"You mean you had to shoot somebody?" Frank asked, his eyes wide.

"It was either me shoot them or have them shoot me, Frank," Longarm told the boy.

"Dad, were you with Marshal Long when the shooting was going on?" Frank asked Greg.

His voice showing his uneasiness, Blanchard replied, "I wasn't very far away."

Seeing what was coming, Longarm spoke quickly. "I asked your daddy to stay back, Frank. He wasn't carrying a gun, and it was my job to take care of them three outlaws."

"Now, Frank, I think you've asked Marshal Long enough questions," Essie said firmly. "The coffee's hot, and we've got enough of our own problems to talk about instead of something that's over and done with." She picked up the coffeepot and filled the cups, passed them around, and settled down into one of the chairs that stood beside the table.

Greg broke the silence that followed. "Longarm's going to spend a couple of days scouting around, Essie. While he's learning the country, I'm going to stay close here and catch up with the work I'm behind on."

Zenia faced Longarm and asked, "What will you be looking for? Sick cattle?"

"I don't rightly know what I'm looking for yet, Zenia," he told her. "From what Greg says, you ain't sure just what's been killing them critters you seen floating downriver."

"I suppose he's told you what I think it is?" Zenia asked.

"Sure. And I don't know all that much about anthrax, but I misdoubt that's what's killing 'em. If it was, there'd likely be more than one at a time coming downstream."

Zenia shook her head. "Not necessarily. There aren't any big herds around here yet, and the area where they're picking up the infection could be very small."

"Greg, you told me coming down from Denver that there's not too many other ranches hereabouts, outside of that big one that Colonel Goodnight just bought," Longarm said. "But now that I've got a fresh look at the land hereabouts, I been wondering about some of the old Spanish spreads that might've been abandoned up in the higher country. Do you know if there might be a few little herds of wild cattle wandering around up on the sides of the mountains? You know, some of 'em might've drifted down to your place here."

"I suppose it's possible," Greg replied. "I know there's a lot of land up there that belongs to some of the Spanish families that settled here way back when. They got spooked out when the Indians rose up against 'em a couple of hundred years ago, and went back to Spain, but they still hold title to the land."

"Well, that's one thing I'll need to find out," Longarm went on thoughtfully.

"Just a friendly tip, Longarm," Greg said. "If I was going to poke around very much hereabouts, I'd keep my eyes peeled and look behind me once in a while."

"I appreciate the tip, Greg, but I've prowled around in just about everyplace west of the Mississippi, and I guess I've run into just about every kind of wild critter there is at one time or the other."

"I'm not worried about wild animals," Greg replied. "But about you disappearing up in the high country."

"You got to be joshing me, Greg," Longarm replied. "I've prowled all over the mountains in a lot of places out here and always managed to come back on my own two feet."

Greg shook his head, and suddenly Longarm realized that he was not joking. Very soberly the rancher asked, "Did you ever hear about the Penitentes?"

"Can't say I have."

"Very few people have, outside of this part of New Mexico Territory."

"Maybe you better tell me about 'em," Longarm suggested.

43

"They're a religious group," the rancher replied. "An off-shoot from the church. They've got a few little churches of their own, *moradas* they call them, tucked away up in the mountains around here."

"Well, now, a church don't sound real bad to me, even if I don't go inside one very often."

"They're not bad people in the sense you mean," Greg went on. "It's just that part of their religion calls for them to hold a ceremony every year around Easter that's sort of an imitation of the Lord's crucifixion. Sometimes the man they crucify dies, and they bury him up there. He just disappears, and nobody ever asks any questions about where he went or why he didn't come back."

"I ain't going up there to look for churches or graves," Longarm pointed out.

"No, but you might stumble onto something they wouldn't want you to see. I understand that if you run across a grave or accidentally stumble onto one of their *moradas*, they'll find out and hunt you down and kill you."

"Dogged if I don't think you really believe what you been telling me, Greg!" Longarm exclaimed.

"I do," Greg said soberly. "Every three or four years around these parts, there's a man who goes up into the mountains and nobody ever sees or hears from him again. When people ask what happened to him, whoever they asked just whispers 'Penitentes,' and that's all they need to say."

"Well, don't worry, I'll keep my eyes peeled," Longarm promised.

The others had been sitting silently, listening to the conversation. Now Essie said, "Greg, I think you've talked long enough. You and the marshal and Frank go look after the horses while Zenia and I get supper on the table." As Longarm passed her on the way out, she dropped her voice and said, "Don't ever believe Greg was joking with you, Marshal. Every word he said is true. If you go up into the Sangre de Cristos, or even when you're riding off alone in the foothills, you'd better be real careful."

Chapter 6

"Before I went off to sleep last night, I got to thinking about that plan I came up with yesterday, Greg," Longarm said the following morning as he and the rancher walked toward the barn to saddle up. "It doesn't look as good to me this morning as it did last night."

They had just finished breakfast and Longarm lifted his hand to reach for a cigar. By habit he groped for the lapel of his coat to reach for the inner breast pocket, before remembering that he had decided to wear only a vest over his grey flannel shirt. He found his cigars in an upper vest pocket, flicked a thumbnail over a match, and lighted the long, slim cheroot. A trail of smoke followed the two men briefly before it dissipated in the clear pre-sunrise air.

"Your scheme sounded all right to me," Greg told him. "Like you said, you've got to learn the lay of the land before you can do much of anything."

"Sure, but that ain't no reason for me to go prowling up in the high country where there's such a little bit of grazing land. I can look around up there later, if I don't run across any leads closer by. Anyhow, instead of going up in the mountains first, I decided it'd be better for me to spend a day or two back-tracking along the Rio Diablo."

"My little story about the Penitentes didn't bother you, did it?" the rancher asked. His back toward Longarm, Greg was smoothing out the saddle blanket on his horse's back.

Longarm shook his head. "I don't scare easy. But while I was thinking things over after I got in my bedroll last night, it just made more sense to see if I can't get a look at one or two of the steer carcasses first, before I begin working up the river trying to find out where they're coming from."

"Well, I wish you luck," Greg said. "I've tried to find the place where they're dumped in the stream, but so far I haven't been able to."

"If you'll just aim me in the general direction of where I need to be heading, I'll see if my luck's any better'n yours," Longarm said, bending down to adjust a strap.

"Starting you off won't be much of a job, now that you're here and can see what I was telling you about yesterday. My spread's all east of the Santa Fe right-of-way, and outside of a few humps here and there it all slopes east, too."

Longarm nodded. "When we rode in from that little whistle stop last night, we kept slanting northeast."

"That's right. Now, there's an old army supply road up north, and it pretty much follows Vermijo Creek, which is my north border. The Mora River's the south border, and right in between is the Rio Diablo. It flows more south than east, and runs into the Mora River down close to Watrous."

"I oughta be able to remember that," Longarm nodded.

"You won't have any trouble. It's all good, level grassland. You can see a good ways ahead of you, and there's not any big thickets or canyons of any size to throw you off. I'd go with you, or send my boy, but I'm going to need him to help me all day today."

"You'll be working along the Diablo part of the time, won't you? I sorta figured you and Frank might keep an eye on it."

"We'll be downstream, yes. Depending on how fast you move, you might run into us."

"I aim to take my time. I'll work back and forth across the country on both sides of the river. I don't guess it's got any anthrax germs in it?"

"Don't worry about the river," Greg said. "Zenia's so worked up about one of us messing around with those steer carcasses that she spends most of her time watching for them."

"I'll scout along the bank like I figured, then," Longarm said. He gave his reins a final twitch and looped them around his hand, ready to lead the livery horse outside.

"Good. I haven't spent much time up on the north part of my range lately, so if you run into any strays you'll be doing me a favor if you chouse them around and get them moving south toward the herd."

"Be glad to," Longarm nodded as he swung into the saddle. "I'll keep an eye on the sun and be back in time for supper."

With a wave, Longarm toed his mount into motion and moved off. He rode through the quiet morning air at an easy gait not hurrying, taking time to get the smell and the feel of the land. Before he had covered much more than a mile the hump of a gentle ridge hid the ranch house from sight. Ahead the grasses rippled in the breeze that sunrise was bringing.

Longarm let his reins go almost completely slack as the horse picked its way down the almost imperceptible slope. From time to time, going by the general description of the terrain that Greg Blanchard had given him, he corrected the animal's inclination to follow the downslope instead of cutting across it diagonally, and as the sun broke the rim of the horizon he saw the glint of water ahead.

That'd be the Rio Diablo, old son, he told himself silently, twisting in the saddle to look back and find a bearing that would serve to guide him on his return. A clump of manzanita he had passed a quarter of an hour earlier gave him a landmark and he tucked away in his mind the silhouetted shape of the lopsided, many-branched shrub before it was lost to sight as he descended the slope that led to the river.

Rio Diablo was like most of the small streams Longarm had seen on the long slopes that dominated the northeastern quadrant of New Mexico Territory. It rushed over a rocky bed from the heights, dashing in repeated cascades, until it reached the point where the land was no longer rocky and broken, where the mountains gave way to an immense alluvial plain that at one time, before some unimaginably vast upheaval took place, had been an inland sea.

Here, where the last rising flanks of the Sangre de Cristo Mountains ended, the short grass country began. The grass would not root on the slopes of the mountains; their soil was too poor, too rocky, and too dry. However, where the waters of the ancient inland sea had once ended, the short grass was rooted thick. It covered the ground downslope for mile after mile even after the terrain to the east became flatter and flatter, and as the land's slope decreased, the current of the rivers grew more and more sluggish.

Longarm judged that he had reached the stream at about the midpoint of the current's changed character. The river was not more than fifty or sixty yards wide and its current was slow. It flowed only fast enough to create a series of tiny surface ripples. From his travel across the eastern section of the short grass area, Longarm knew that the streams would spread wider and grow more and more shallow in their slow eastward flow toward the Canadian. Here, the river's bottom looked like solid sand, but Longarm had seen such riverbeds before and did not trust them. He knew that the level, innocent-looking streambed harbored quicksand as well as solid sand.

Turning his horse, he rode upriver, keeping close to the water's edge, until he found a rocky outcrop that stretched from one bank to the other. Longarm reined his mount into the water and let the animal gingerly pick its own way across the stones to the opposite bank. He stopped then and let the horse drink while he lighted another cheroot and turned his eyes upstream.

In the cool morning, the air had not yet formed the shivering heat waves that would form later in the day. As the sun's heat increased, the cool air from the grass roots would rise and form ripples. These would begin in the early afternoon and once they had started would remain until sundown, blurring a man's vision until he could make out details for only a mile or two ahead. Now the air was like crystal, and Longarm could see the roof ridges of the few houses in Valmora that had been built above the rest of the town on the mountain flanks.

There sure ain't no cattle between here and there, old son, he told himself. *So if there's some ground around here that's infecting steers with anthrax, it's bound to be downriver.* He twitched the reins to turn his horse and started riding slowly downstream at the water's edge.

He had covered a mile or two, dividing his attention between the river's bottom, its banks, and the wide, sweeping curves in its bed ahead, when he saw the first sign of something that looked out of place. Longarm did not know at first why the patch of riverbank had drawn his attention, and decided he had better find out. He reined in to study it more closely.

To his searching eyes, there was something alien about an area roughly fifteen or twenty feet in diameter. It stood ten or a dozen paces from the water's edge and was roughly circular in shape, its hue somehow disturbing. At its center the ocher-colored ground matched the ground which ran back from the stone-studded riverbank to where the sea of short grass began, but there was a belt of earth around this section which was much darker than the soil visible between the stones that thrust up from the ground between the circle and the water's edge.

Now, that just don't look natural, old son, Longarm thought as he gazed at the alien-looking patch of ground.

Dropping the reins of his horse so the animal would stand, he swung out of his saddle and walked up to the edge of the disturbed area. At close range, it was easy for him to see that the circular area had been dug up and then re-covered carefully. Within another day or two the moisture that caused the disturbed area to look different would have been sucked up by the dry air and the spot would have blended into its surroundings.

Now, the kind of folks that live around here has got enough work to keep 'em busy, Longarm considered. *They wouldn't be digging up a place like that without a reason, and when somebody digs a hole like that one and covers it up so careful, the reason's generally that they got something to hide. But that ground don't look like it's got too hard yet, and what's been dug up once can be dug up again.*

A few minutes of scouting around in a pile of tangled brush deposited by the river when it had been high turned up a manzanita branch with a gnarled fork at one end. Sacrificing one of his saddle strings, Longarm wound twigs across the vee of the branch and secured them with the leather thong to make a crude but usable shovel. He started digging at the edge of the circle, his makeshift shovel easily lifting away the friable soil.

He had removed only a few inches of the loose dirt before his improvised digging tool scraped on stone. Longarm stopped work while he took stock of the small area he had uncovered. That the rock lying below the thin layer of dirt had not come

49

from the riverbed was obvious at a glance. Its surface showed no signs of having been worn smooth by the scouring of many years' exposure to the abrasive action of a streambed's silt-filled waters. It was rough to his touch when he passed his fingertips over it.

Somebody's put this thing here, old son, he told himself as he stroked the stone. *And not too long ago, from the way this hole looks. Now, it don't take much figuring to work out that they'd have a reason. The question's what that reason was.*

Picking up his makeshift shovel again, Longarm went back to lifting the soil away from the buried stone. Ten minutes' work bared its edges. They rested on other stones. Tapping with the butt of the manzanita branch on the slab he had uncovered produced a hollow sound.

"Looks like there might be a cave of some sort under here," Longarm muttered aloud. "But it's gonna to take a lot more work to lift up that slab of rock and find out."

A few more minutes of scouting in the high-water litter uncovered a length of tree limb long enough and sturdy enough to be used as a lever. Another short period of searching, this time along the river's edge, led to his finding a chunk of stone big enough to support the lever.

Muscling the stone to the spot where it was needed, Longarm worked his improvised lever under the edge of the slab and shoved down. The slab did not move. He tried again, and this time the slab shifted a fraction of an inch. Encouraged at even such a small bit of progress, Longarm crouched beside the end of the lever, grasped it firmly in both hands, and leaped upward, putting his full weight on the branch.

A rasping of rocks grating under the surface of the ground sounded as Longarm's feet rose into the air and the branch bent under the strain. It started slipping downward, as if someone were tugging hard on its opposite end. The ground trembled and hidden stones rasped abrasively. Then Longarm's feet jolted down. The loose soil shook when he tried to dig his boot heels in. Then, as he bent his knees in an effort to leap away, the earth beneath his scrabbling feet gave way and threw him off balance.

With a dull, clattering crash the stone he had been levering up cracked and split. As the ground opened under his feet Longarm dropped the manzanita branch and threw his arms wide, swinging them in an effort to keep his balance. Half the flat stone that had covered the black hole suddenly dropped away. The ground gaped under Longarm's boot soles and dropped away. He began to slip down into the hole despite his efforts to hold himself in place. He spread his arms, flinging them wide, trying to arrest his sudden plunge, but the weight of his body was too great for the belated effort to be effective.

Longarm plunged down into blackness. The remainder of the flat stone on which one of his arms had been resting flipped over. The broken edge of the falling slab brushed from beneath his arm and flipped across his shoulder. The stone careened in its inexorable path. The edge crashed into the side of Longarm's head. He was conscious of a split second of sudden, blinding pain; then he knew nothing more.

Awareness that he was lying on a cold, rough surface trickled into Longarm's brain. He opened his eyes to blackness, a darkness he could not penetrate. For a moment he lay without moving, then full consciousness flooded back, but the darkness did not abate. His head was aching, and when he brought up his hand to feel it he realized that he had lost his hat. There was a long, swollen lump over one side of his head above his temple that was tender to his touch.

Then memory returned. Longarm remembered his struggle to pry up the stone slab, recalled it breaking and causing him to fall, but he was still unable to believe the total absence of light. He flicked his eyelids several times, but that did nothing to make the gloom brighten. Slowly, he lifted himself to his feet.

Without really being aware that he was moving his arms and hands, Longarm pulled a cigar from his vest pocket and took out a match. When he flicked his thumb across its head and the match burst into flame the light stabbed into his eyes like a dagger. He closed them and opened them slowly to allow his pupils to adjust, and took stock of his surroundings while he held the flaming match to the end of his cigar.

He could see that he was in some sort of underground cavern, but his eyes had still not fully adjusted to the light and they filmed with tears, distorting his vision. He held the match until it burned down and lighted another at once. This time he could see his surroundings. He looked up. There was no doubt from his first glimpse that the cave in which he stood was at least partly manmade, for its low ceiling was covered with

51

rows of stone in neat, overlapping layers like fish scales.

By the dim reddish light of the flickering match he examined the hole through which he had fallen. It was far above his head, at least four or five feet, well out of reach. As the match flickered and began to burn his fingertips, Longarm belatedly looked around the underground chamber, and by the match's dying flame got a glimpse of a number of oblong bundles laid in neat rows on the floor. Then the match burned down so far that he was forced to drop it as he had the first.

Longarm puffed at his cheroot until the lighted tip glowed bright once more. He peered through the smoke his puffs had raised, trying to estimate the size of the cavity. All that he could determine was that it was oblong in shape. The bundles on the floor could be only one thing: the bodies of dead men wrapped in some kind of rough cloth.

When he realized that he had fallen into what must be a sort of tomb or mausoleum, Longarm shuddered involuntarily. He had no fear of death; he encountered it frequently in the course of carrying out his assigned cases. However, the idea of being confined in a cave that was literally paved with corpses whose numbers he could not yet estimate and whose age he had no way of judging was not especially appealing.

A thunking noise came through the opening above his head and banished thoughts of his surroundings. After a moment Longarm identified the sound. It was his horse tapping a forefoot on the ground. Remembering that he had not tethered the animal, Longarm stepped carefully through the darkness of the underground chamber until he was directly below the hole through which he had fallen. He looked up and saw the stars, seeming as bright as small distant suns in the pitch blackness.

Another whinny came from the horse and Longarm whistled. He heard hoofbeats overhead and the horse neighed. The sound echoed through the cavern in such a way that it sounded as if the animal was standing at his elbow.

Longarm had a fleeting mental picture of the horse stepping into the hole through which he had fallen and called quickly, "Stand! Whoa!"

An answering whinny came through the overhead opening and the sound of the horse's movements stopped. Longarm tried again to stretch his arms high enough to touch the ceiling, knowing as he did so that his gesture was futile.

Too bad you never was much of a one for jumping, old son,

he told himself. *It seems like that's the only way you'll be able to reach that hole. So hunker down and give it a try!*

Crouching, Longarm poised himself for a moment, took a deep breath, and leaped upward. He raised his arms as he rose, his fingers clawed and ready to grasp the rim of the opening. Even as he was rising into the air, Longarm could see that his effort was going to fail. Instinctively, he kicked while still in mid-air, trying to propel himself a few inches higher, but he began falling back while his outstretched hands were still more than a foot below the opening.

Then he was falling back, his feet stinging as he landed heavily on the hard-packed floor of the cavern. He put out a hand and steadied himself to keep from falling against the wall of the chamber, then turned his head upward and stared at the oval opening that outlined a patch of sky. The night's blue-black heaven and brightly twinkling stars seemed to be mocking him.

Seems to me there's some old saying that one swallow don't make a summer, Longarm considered. *Except I never could figure out whether that meant a swallow like a bird or a sip of Tom Moore. But whatever it's supposed to mean, you got to try again. Maybe you'll do better next time.*

Longarm's second leap took him no higher. He was wiser than he'd been before. The faint starshine that trickled in through the hole was bright enough to let him see his upthrust hands, a pair of pale blurs above his head, and he could gauge how much he fell short of gaining the distance needed to grasp the rim of the hole.

You just ain't got it in you to jump as high as you need to, old son, he told himself after his boot soles had hit the floor again. *That hole's a good three feet too high for you ever to reach it. This time you really put yourself up shit creek without a paddle. And that means it's time you quit floundering around like a damned panicked tenderfoot and start figuring out how to get outa this fix you got yourself into.*

Chapter 7

Hunkering down, Longarm took stock of his situation. The weapons which had saved him in other situations were useless to him in this one. The Colt in its cross-draw holster might as well be so much metal. His rifle was out of reach, in the saddle scabbard of his horse, but even had it been in his hand it would be no more useful than the Colt. Item by item, he considered each piece of clothing he wore, from hat to boots, and found nothing that would be effective in getting him out of his predicament.

Nor would the contents of his pockets give him any help. The wallet in one hip pocket of his trousers contained only his identification papers and his badge, pinned inside its fold; the other hip pocket held nothing but a bandanna. His side pockets were equally bare of helpful objects. In one there was the expense money given him by Billy Vail, in the other nothing but his jackknife. The upper pockets of his vest carried cigars and matches; the lower pair held his watch with its chain and

54

his derringer attached to the other end of the chain.

"Might as well face it, old son," he said aloud into the blackness. "You ain't got one blessed thing that's going to help you get outa here. So hold down your craw and start looking at them bodies laying over there. It might be there's something you can use in them blankets they got wrapped around 'em."

Holding a match, his steel-hard thumbnail on its head ready to kindle it into flame, Longarm shuffled across the stone floor of the cavern. A faint glow of starshine from the hole through which he had fallen did not relieve the darkness of the chamber, but provided a patch of less dense dark which he glanced at over his shoulder now and then to be sure he was moving in a straight line. Long ago he had learned how easy it was for a man in pitch darkness to slant off to one side or the other even in the course of taking a step or two.

When the toe of his boot encountered an obstacle, Longarm stopped and hunkered down. He ran his hand across the object which had touched his boot toe, and felt the firm texture of a hand-woven blanket. Pressing harder on the blanket, he moved his fingers slowly over its surface, tracing the contours of the body it concealed.

Even in the pitch blackness, Longarm could identify the contours of a human body, but the blanket could not conceal from his probing fingers that the body's flesh was not elastic and yielding, but had the solid feel of dessicated flesh that lay in a thin layer over a skeleton. Moving his hand very slowly and carefully, he ran it across the long-dead form, then traced the humps made by the corpse's arms, folded across its chest.

As his fingers moved, exploring the shrunken arms, they encountered something that was neither flesh nor bone. He drew his fingertips along the rounded bulge. Whatever the blanket concealed was a long, thin, tubular-shaped object, with another quite similar one crossing it at right angles near the center. Longarm traced it twice before he decided that it must be a large cross which spanned the body of the corpse from chin to crotch and shoulder to shoulder.

"Well, old son," he breathed into the darkness, "even if you ain't exactly a praying man yourself, at least you got enough sense to figure out that whoever put these bodies in here fixed 'em up so they'd be right sure to get to Heaven. And unless you can figure a way to get yourself out, or Greg and his boy get worried and come looking for you, this might just be the time when you'll make that big trip up to the sky."

Working as fast as was possible in the pitch darkness, Longarm found the edge of the blanket in which the corpse was wrapped and pulled it away. He ran his hand over the exposed arms and across the dry, shrunken skin, until he felt the round end of what he was sure was a piece of wood.

Fingering the billet, Longarm guessed it to be a section cut from a sapling or from one of the lower branches of a fairly well developed tree, since the diameter was almost three times that of his forefinger but not as large around as his wrist. He slid his hand along the wood and encountered a bulge made by a number of narrow strips that after several moments of exploring with his fingertips he deduced must be rawhide thongs. The strips of leather were iron-hard, crisscrossed over the surface of the billet.

Probing at the lashing, his hand was stopped by a second piece of wood which the thongs held securely at right angles to the first piece he had touched. A bit more finger exploration and he realized that the wooden pieces formed a cross. As his fingers brushed along the surface of the crosspiece, they encountered a rough spot. Moving them back and forth revealed the roughness to be carving, letters that extended most of the way along the face of the wood.

Longarm tried to read the inscription by following the outline of the letters with a fingertip, but the carving was too small and so shallow that he could not distinguish one letter from another. After he had tried for several minutes to decipher the inscription, the letters still made no sense. He decided to use another of his scanty stock of matches.

Taking one out, he closed his eyes to shield them from the sudden flare that would spurt when he struck it and flicked his thumbnail across the head. The match gave a tiny hiss and as it sputtered into flame its blaze registered red even through Longarm's closed eyelids. After the brilliance had faded to an almost imperceptible glow, Longarm opened his eyes and focused them on the carved words.

"Memoria a Dios de F. Gomez. Los Hermanos Penitentes. 1779," he read in a half whisper, then exclaimed aloud, "Why, that's more'n a hundred years ago! No wonder this fellow's all shrunk and shrivelled up. And likely them others been laying here just about as long."

Looking down at the torso and head, he saw that it must

have been a young man, for the wrinkled face showed no signs of either whiskers or a beard. Time and the arid atmosphere of the cavern had mummified the mortal remains of F. Gomez. The body was little more than a layer of shrunken, leathery skin clinging to the skeleton.

Deep pits marked the eye sockets; the nose of the mummy was truncated where the soft tissue below the bridge had shrivelled; the drawn-in lips revealed two rows of yellowed teeth; and the chin below them was only a bit wider than Longarm's thumb. When he had pulled away the blanket that had shrouded the corpse for a century, he had bared part of its torso. On the crossed arms and exposed rib cage the dark, leathery, puckered skin clung as close to the skeleton as did that which covered the skull.

While part of Longarm's mind had been occupied by reading the inscription carved on the cross and examining the mummified torso, another part was signalling to him that he needed to look again around the subterranean chamber while the match still burned. He glanced quickly across the floor of the cavern. In addition to the body on which he'd been concentrating his attention, there were eleven other blanket-wrapped forms lying head to toe in neat rows that stretched from one side of the cavern to the other.

And I'll bet that every one of them is just like this one here, Longarm told himself silently as the match began burning his fingers. He flicked his hand quickly to extinguish the match and darkness once more shrouded the underground chamber. He lowered the mummified figure he had been holding to let it rest on the floor again and stood up. His thoughts ran on, *Except the years carved on the crosses wouldn't all be the same. From what Greg was saying, the Penitentes only have their ceremony once a year.*

Force of habit led Longarm's fingers to the vest pocket in which he carried his cigars. Without really thinking of what he was doing, he slid one of the cheroots from his pocket and took out a match. His thumbnail was resting on the match head before he realized that he was being very prodigal with both matches and cigars.

You just better put off having another smoke right now, old son, he advised himself silently. *If you get stuck down here very long, you'll be wanting matches and cigars later on a lot more'n you do right now.*

From above he heard the horse whinny again. Turning away from the rows of bodies, Longarm groped his way to the wall of the chamber and followed it until he felt a faint current of fresh air. He looked up. There were stars outlining the rim of the hole, and he could hear the horse shifting its hooves on the ground above.

"Just stand where you're at, Calceta," he called to the animal. "I'll be outa here by hook or by crook, soon as I can figure a way, and we'll be moving along."

Except that ain't going to be real soon, he went on to himself. *It's too bad this cross is too short to use for a ladder; if it was longer, I'd be outa here in a jiffy.*

Even as his wishful thought was fading, a new one took shape in Longarm's mind. *Now, hold up here, old son. If you didn't have but one cross, you'd be stuck. But chances are there's a cross in every one of them bundles. And you got the blankets, too. They'd be easy to cut into strips, and tight as them blankets is woven they're good as rope. Then all you got to do is tie three or four of the crosses together and make yourself a ladder.*

Action replaced thought within seconds. Longarm stepped back to the corpse he had partly uncovered and took out his pocketknife. Lifting the cross from the body's chest, he laid it on the cavern floor and felt his way to the next mummified form. Just as he had hoped, his probing fingers traced the shape of a cross almost identical to the first under the blanket that swathed the stiff figure.

Now, before you get your hopes up too high, old son, you better test this out a little bit, he cautioned himself.

Holding one end of the long shaft of the cross on the floor, he lifted one booted foot and placed it on the cross piece, then leaned forward and put the weight of his body on the ancient wood. The leather thongs that bound the pieces together creaked in protest, but the crosspiece did not slip or give way.

Encouraged by his successful test, Longarm started to work in earnest. Within ten minutes he had found and removed half a dozen more of the wooden crosses from the mummies. Laying them on the cavern floor, he aligned them by feel, overlapping the long end of one with the short end of the next.

Then he took the blanket he had removed from the first body and began cutting it into strips. The tough raw woolen yarn was hard to slice through. It resisted even the razor-sharp blade of his pocketknife. The strips of woven wool he produced were ragged and uneven, but they did not give when he tried to stretch them. After he had cut up two of the blankets he started wrapping the improvised rope around the overlapped ends of the crosses.

In the dense black of the cavern, where he could see nothing of what he was doing, Longarm had to work by feel. Wrapping the overlapping pieces of wood together was slow work, for the strips of woven wool had a tendency to curl and twist as he wound them around the wooden shafts. Patiently he straightened the twists and smoothed the strips and wrapped them closely together around the doubled shafts, then reversed the direction of his wrapping and tied the ends together.

Longarm did not try to keep track of the time while he struggled to improvise a ladder. He kept at his task steadily, wrapping the ends of the crosses together firmly, pulling each turn taut, checking every knot twice, knowing that if the ladder he was trying to create broke under his weight he would have the whole job to do over again.

By the time he had knotted the last strips together, his knees were aching from their long pressure against the stone-hard earth of the cavern's floor, and his finger joints were growing stiff from the continued hard tugging that was required to tighten the knots in his makeshift ropes.

Rising to his feet, Longarm flexed some of the stiffness out of his hands by clenching them several times. He stomped hard on the cavern floor to loosen up his aching knees. He had denied himself the luxury of a cigar while he was working, and now he fished one of the long, thin cheroots from his pocket. He puffed his cigar into a glowing coal as quickly as possible, then used the short time remaining before the match began scorching his fingertips to inspect the ladder.

"It looks about as good as I got any right to expect," he said aloud as the match burned his fingertips. He blew it out and the cavern was again plunged into darkness. "Seeing as I had to work blind and didn't have no real rope to use. Now the next ten miles down the road is finding out how good it's going to work."

Never a man to delay action, Longarm picked up his improvised construction and carried it to the gap in the ceiling. He used the starlight that outlined the hole to place the ladder. It reached the top rim of the hole with an inch or so to spare.

Longarm leaned against it gingerly at first, then more heavily. When it creaked and bent under the pressure of his body, he took a backward step and started climbing.

He had mounted the first two steps and his head was level with the cavern's ceiling when one of the wrappings at the level of his waist popped and the frail device began to quiver. Longarm felt it starting to give way. He found the next crosspiece with his foot and kicked hard just as the ladder sagged under him. His kick propelled Longarm high enough for his head and shoulders to emerge into the starlit night above the opening.

As the bottom rungs swung free, he spread his arms wide and lurched forward, bending at the waist and clawing at the roots of the short grass to hold himself in place. The top of the ladder was sliding back into the cavern, but Longarm had enough momentum to carry his torso forward the few inches necessary to sprawl with his chest on the ground, and to hold himself in place when the ladder fell away.

While half of his body dangled in mid-air, Longarm started pulling himself the rest of the way out of the hole. His fingers clawed and dug into the ground, his arms extended full-length. He rested his elbows on the soil and used them as levers while he finished extricating himself. His legs emerged from the hole and he rolled away from it while the noise of the ladder collapsing was still echoing in the quiet air.

"Now, that's something you don't wanta have to do more'n once, old son," Longarm said aloud. Hearing his voice, the horse greeted him with a whinny and started moving toward him. "Just stand where you are, Calceta," Longarm commanded the animal. The livery horse stopped obediently and pawed the soil with one foot while Longarm stood up and looked around.

After the deep blackness of the underground chamber, the starlit night seemed almost as bright as day, and as he glanced around Longarm realized with something of a shock that day was not far off. To the east he could see the first indication that night was fading. For a short distance above the line of the horizon the stars were invisible now, and a thin line of grey separated the dark sky from the horizon's rim.

"It sure don't seem like falling such a little ways could've knocked you out all that time, old son," Longarm muttered under his breath. He took out his watch and glanced at it, discovered that it was almost four o'clock, and shook his head.

"But it looks like that's what it done. Of course, it took you a while to figure your way outa that hole, too."

Longarm stepped to the gap through which he had emerged and looked at it, trying to decide whether to leave the yawning black hole exposed and trust that no one would discover it, or to take the time to cover it temporarily until he could return with a lantern and a real ladder to make a more thorough investigation. A growl from his stomach decided him. He swung into the saddle and toed the horse back toward the Blanchard ranch.

At the little stream he had splashed across the previous day, the horse whinnied, and Longarm realized that the animal had gone part of a day and a full night without drinking. He reined in to let it drink, and moved a few paces upstream to scoop up a few swallows of water himself. Mounting again, he reined his horse across the stream and up the gentle slant of its bed onto the prairie.

Since he had swallowed those few sips of water, Longarm's empty stomach had begun sending him sharp reminders. His fingers moved to his vest pocket for a cheroot to quiet his hunger pangs. He had the cigar in his hand and was closing his mouth on its end when he glanced across the broad stretch of rangeland that lay between him and the ranch. The low-hanging moon was just beginning to fade now, and the thin line of paling darkness that outlined the horizon had grown perceptibly brighter.

Longarm's eyes had been attuned to the darkness by his long stay in the cave. Midway between the place where he was and the rim of light he caught a glimpse of movement.

Slitting his eyelids, Longarm stared fixedly at the spot where he had seen the almost imperceptible motion. For a moment his eyes did not respond. Then suddenly his vision cleared and he could see that what had attracted his attention was a trio of horses moving slowly across the range.

They were too far away for him to make out anything except their slowly advancing forms. As his eyes adjusted to the distance he could see that two of the horses bore riders on their backs while the third was a led horse carrying a tarpaulin-shrouded load. The load was long and narrow and sagged over the horse's back. The burden looked enough like a corpse to bring an instinctive reaction from any lawman. *Old son,* Longarm told himself, *them fellows ain't hauling that load across*

61

the prairie at this time of day just to keep their faces from getting sunburnt. There ain't a place close enough for them to've started from any time before midnight. Whatever it is they're up to, they don't want nobody seeing what's on the back of that led horse. And that's just the kind of load you better go take a look at.

Longarm toed Calceta's flank, and the horse moved off. The two night riders could now see Longarm only if they turned and looked over their shoulders in the direction from which he was approaching.

Gambling that they would keep moving in the same direction they were now headed, Longarm did not urge his horse into a gallop. He kneed Calceta into a fast walk that covered distance fairly quickly without the giveaway drumbeat the animal's hooves would produce if he tried to move faster. On the bare prairie, with no close cover ahead or on either side, he hoped he would be able to get close enough to see the pair more plainly before the hoofbeats of his mount gave away his pursuit.

His plan was reasonable, and it might have worked if one of the men ahead had not turned to look back. Longarm was too close to them now to miss being spotted. The rider who had looked back turned to his companion, who glanced around in turn. Then the pair put the spurs to their horses.

Longarm dug his boot heels into Calceta's flank. One of the riders ahead twisted in his saddle and let off a pair of quick revolver shots. The range was still too great for accurate shooting with a pistol, and Longarm did not bother to swerve out of his path to try to avoid the fleeing man's bullets. He was also too old a hand at running gunfights to bring out a rifle and try to use it while moving at a gallop.

Drawing his Colt, he snapshotted once, a warning shot. He knew his voice would not carry to the fleeing riders, but to fulfill his standing orders Longarm shouted, "You men pull up! I'm a deputy United States marshal and I got some questions to ask you!"

As he had anticipated, the men ahead paid no attention to his shout. Holstering his Colt until he could come within range, Longarm bent forward in the saddle and kept up his chase.

Chapter 8

Now Longarm saw the second rider sliding a rifle out of his saddle holster. Waiting until the fleeing man twisted around in his saddle and shouldered the weapon, Longarm let off another round from his Colt, but the range was still too great for the handgun's slug to carry accurately.

Muzzle-blast spurted red from the rifle the second rider had brought to bear. Longarm's horse shrilled a high-pitched whinny of pain and broke stride. It hobbled on for a moment or two, turning to one side as it moved, favoring its left rear hoof.

Another bullet from the rifle thunked into the dirt only a yard away as the horse stumbled clumsily and stopped. Glancing down, Longarm saw that the horse had lifted its off hind leg from the ground. The rifle slug had hit Calceta's hoof just above its metal shoe, and the horse was holding its leg up. The shoe had been knocked halfway off and a big chip was missing from the hoof.

It was obvious that the animal was not going to be able to

keep up the chase. Longarm holstered his Colt, let the reins drop free, and slipped out of his saddle.

Ahead, the second rider had drawn his rifle from its saddle sheath and was bringing it up to fire. Longarm grabbed Calceta's reins. He twisted and yanked and the horse fell to the ground. Pulling his Winchester out of its scabbard, Longarm took quick aim at the man who had just fired. He squeezed off a shot. The rider swayed, but did not fall.

Longarm saw the second man bring up his rifle and turned his attention to this new threat, but while he was swinging his own weapon to cover the new threat the man's companion got off a shot that whistled uncomfortably close as it passed Longarm's head. Involuntarily, Longarm flinched as the rifle slug sang its wicked message so close to his ear, and the shot intended for the other rider went wide.

Longarm began snapshooting, working the Winchester's lever as fast as he could. He sent four unaimed shots in the general direction of the two horsemen, and when he dropped his cheek to the stock for an aimed shot he saw over the vee of his rear sight that the men had speeded up.

One of them was bending forward over the neck of his mount, and Longarm was sure that at least one of his shots had scored a hit. The second was still twisted sideways in his saddle, his rifle shouldered. In the improving light Longarm got a fleeting glimpse of a swarthy moustached face before a puff of powder smoke spurted from the muzzle. As Longarm dropped flat, the puff was followed by the high-pitched report of the rifle. The bullet cut the air above Longarm's head in the space where he had been standing a split second earlier.

After disabling Longarm's horse, the riders ahead had stepped up their pace in spite of the exchange of gunfire. Though only a few moments had passed since Longarm had been forced to end his pursuit, the riders were uncertain targets now, even though the steadily brightening sky outlined them more clearly. More interested in escaping than in trading shots, they were galloping steadily away. The one who had been hugging his horse's neck was once more erect in the saddle, and to make themselves trickier targets they had also begun to zigzag, dragging the led horse with its load behind them.

Though he knew it was chancy shooting in the constantly changing dawnlight, Longarm sharpened his aim and fired again, but missed. Before he could tighten his aim for another shot, the riders and the horse they were leading dropped out of sight behind one of the ledges that cut across the prairie.

Longarm got to his feet, his lips crimped in a line of grim dissatisfaction, gazing at the spot where the pair had vanished below the horizon. There was no landmark by which he could identify the place where they had disappeared, and no way of knowing in which direction they might turn after they had gotten safely out of sight. With a disgusted shrug, he turned his attention to his crippled horse.

Though he had resigned himself to a long walk back to the Blanchard place, Longarm brightened a bit when he hunkered down for a close examination of Calceta's hoof. The shoe was dangling on one side, but the rifle slug had not bent the metal. The shoe had been pulled away unevenly from the hoof by the bullet's impact, but none of the nails were lost. After he had studied the hoof for a moment, Longarm rose to his feet and started walking in a zigzag pattern away from the horse, pushing the grass aside with his feet, his eyes searching the ground.

After he had looked unsuccessfully for several minutes, he found what he'd been searching for: a rock big enough to hammer the horseshoe nails in again, but small enough to fit into the palm of his hand. Kicking the rock free of the soil in which it was half buried, Longarm carried it back to where Calceta was standing. He lifted the injured hoof and the horse whinnied worriedly.

"You ain't got nothing to worry about," Longarm said. "I ain't going to hurt you any more'n a blacksmith would."

Straddling Calceta's hind leg, Longarm pulled the hoof up between his thighs and clamped them closed on the horse's leg just above the fetlock joint. Grasping the hoof in his left hand, he bent it upward as far as possible and began hammering the loosened horseshoe nails in with his improvised hammer. The horse whinnied and neighed once or twice while Longarm was working, but it had been shod in blacksmith shops enough times to be familiar with the routine. It stood calmly enough, snorting now and then, while Longarm tapped the nails back into place.

"There, now," he said after he had driven the last nail home. Dropping the rock, he walked around to the horse's head and picked up the dangling reins. "Let's see if you can walk easy."

Although the animal favored the hoof that had been clipped by the bullet, it walked readily enough. Longarm led it for a short distance, keeping an eye on its torn hoof, and when he was sure that it would cause no immediate problem, swung into the saddle and turned toward the ranch house.

As soon as the horse settled down to a steady pace Longarm took a cigar out of his pocket and lighted it. The smoke from the cheroot trailed over his shoulder, a grey wisp in the golden rays of the rising sun, as he rode on slowly through the steadily brightening day.

Even from a distance, Longarm could tell that something unusual must be going on at the Blanchard ranch. It was late morning, for he'd been forced to let his horse set its own slow pace. The sun was high in the sky, almost midway between the horizon and its zenith when he came in sight of the ranch house. There were two horses standing in front of the big barn. One was bareback, and Frank was saddling the second. As Longarm drew closer, Greg came out with a saddle for the second horse.

Essie Blanchard rushed from the house carrying a bundle which she tried to get Frank to take, but he kept shaking his head and turned back to his saddling job. Greg had thrown the saddle he carried onto the back of the second horse. Essie went to Frank and offered the bundle to him, but he also waved her away. She was left standing beside the horses, both Greg and Frank ignoring her as they worked, until Zenia came out and joined them.

Zenia went to Greg's side and began talking to him. Even from a distance Longarm could tell from Greg's headshakes and gestures that he was trying to get her to move away from him. Then the two women became involved in a conversation which did not end until Frank turned to his father. Essie and Zenia broke off their talk and joined the men. It was easy for Longarm to see from their excited gestures that all four were trying to talk at the same time.

Longarm was close enough to the barn by then to raise his voice and hail them. His shout of greeting broke up the conclave as Greg, Essie, Zenia, and Frank turned to look at him. Then all four started running to meet him.

"What happened to you?" Greg called as soon as he was close enough. He indicated the limping horse and went on, "I hope you didn't run into trouble."

"All of us thought you'd gotten thrown, or hurt some way," Zenia added almost before Greg had finished speaking.

"We were really worried about you when you didn't get back here last night, Marshal Long," Essie chimed in.

"At least Ma was," Frank said, a smile wreathing his young face. "Dad and I couldn't get her to believe you weren't lying hurt somewhere out on the range."

"Well, it makes me feel good to know somebody was thinking about me," Longarm told them. He decided that until he had talked privately to Greg there was no reason to upset the women and the boy by telling the whole story. "I just ran into a few things that kept me busy till it was a mite late to start back last night, me not knowing the country hereabouts."

"I'll bet you're just starved!" Essie said. "Zenia, why don't you come along and give me a hand so we can get Marshal Long some breakfast real quick."

Greg waited until the two women were out of earshot, then he asked Longarm, "You feel like telling me who shot the shoe off your horse?"

"I'd sure be glad to if I was able to," Longarm replied. "That'd mean I'd know myself."

"Somebody just started shooting at you?"

"Two of 'em. They was riding across that stretch of range up to the north, just this side of the river."

"You're talking about the Rio Diablo?" Greg asked.

Longarm nodded. "I got to the other side of it, but I had to stop to check on something I'd stumbled onto. I never did get all the way to Vermijo Creek. I was on my way back here to the ranch when I ran into 'em."

"And they just started shooting for no reason at all?"

"Oh, I hailed 'em and told 'em I wanted to talk."

"I don't suppose you gave them any reason to shoot?"

"I got a hunch that me seeing 'em with a led horse carrying a big tarp-wrapped load was all the reason they needed," Longarm replied seriously.

"What kind of load?"

"Like I said, it was all bundled up in a tarp."

"And you couldn't guess what it was?"

"It was just at daybreak, Greg. The light was awful bad and I couldn't rightly tell, because I didn't get all that close to them two fellows."

"You figure it was a body?"

Longarm said thoughtfully, "That's what occurred to me when I spotted it. Then they began shooting and I didn't pay all that much attention to anything except their guns."

"Was it big enough to be a steer?"

"Not a full-grown one," Longarm replied, shaking his head. "I guess maybe it could've been a yearling with its legs tied up tight against its belly."

"It's too bad they hit your horse before you got close enough to them to make sure."

"I'd give a pretty if I was sure. Since I ain't, I'd just as soon play my cards up against my chest and not make any kind of a guess."

"Well, that's your business, of course," Greg replied a bit stiffly.

"I ain't aiming to keep anything from you, Greg," Longarm said quickly. "As soon as I find out something that I'm certain about, you'll know it right away."

"You've got your own way of handling a case, I know," Greg said. His voice showed that he had been mollified by Longarm's promise. He went on, "If I know my Essie, she and Zenia will have some grub on the table by now. I was going to take Frank and go try to find you, but now that you're back, I suppose we'd better go finish the job we started yesterday. Unless you need us to help you, that is."

"I thank you kindly for offering, Greg," Longarm replied. "But right now I'm just looking for loose strings to pull. Soon as I get a better idea of what's going on, I'll sure be asking you for some help."

Greg nodded his satisfaction and Longarm went into the house. Essie and Zenia had set a place at the long trestle table and Essie was just dishing up slices of bacon to go with the steaming flapjacks on the platter that stood on a corner of the kitchen range.

"Sit down, Marshal Long," Zenia said. "We've got breakfast ready for you."

Longarm settled into his chair. The smell of just-cooked bacon was reminding him how hungry he was.

Zenia put the plate in front of him. "Now, just go right ahead and eat off the platter," she said. "That's what Greg always likes to do when he has a late meal."

Longarm began eating. After he had taken a few bites, he looked up and noticed that Essie and Zenia were still standing, watching him eat.

"You know, I eat so many meals by myself that I'd sure enjoy it if you ladies would set down with me," he said. "Maybe you'd have a cup of coffee, just to keep me company."

"I guess we could stand one, at that," Essie nodded. She looked at Zenia. "Get the cups. I'll bring the coffeepot to the table. Marshal Long will likely want some more."

After the sisters had settled down, Zenia said to Longarm, "We never did hear you say what kept you out all night. I hope it wasn't anything bad."

"I set out on a trail and it kept me going longer than I'd figured on," Longarm told them, adhering to the strict truth without elaborating on details. "I guess you'd say I sorta got sidetracked. It wasn't such a much. In my business, things like that happen."

"Then you weren't in any trouble?" Essie asked.

"Nothing I couldn't handle," he said. "Like you see, I got back here all right."

"What about the trail you were following?" Zenia frowned.

"Oh, it'll still be there when I get back to it," Longarm answered, keeping his voice casual. "Except it'll be a little while before I can do that. I got to ride into Valmora soon as I finish eating. That livery horse I rented has a loose shoe, and if I don't get it tended to it'll be bound to give me trouble later on."

"When do you plan to start keeping watch on the river?" Zenia asked. "After all, that's what you came here for . . . to find out why somebody keeps throwing steer carcasses into it."

"And you're sure them steer carcasses that you've seen float downstream are infected with anthrax," Longarm said.

"I certainly am!" Zenia exclaimed a bit indignantly. "Why, I wouldn't go near one for any amount of money, and I've warned Essie and Greg and Frank not to get close to them, either."

"Maybe I ain't smart enough to figure this out myself," Longarm frowned. "And I don't recall that I ever seen a steer that had anthrax. But if you don't get close to a dead steer's carcass, and can't touch it to look for signs of what killed it, how can you tell it died from anthrax?"

Zenia was silent for a moment, frowning thoughtfully. Then she said, "Why, you can generally tell because the carcass will be swollen up, bloated. And the dead steer will have some traces of dried blood on its muzzle."

"It seems to me that if a steer with blood on its nose begun floating down a river, the water'd wash away the blood in pretty short order," Longarm objected, his voice mild.

"It'd still be bloated, though," Zenia insisted.

"Even if I give you that, Zenia, when a critter keels over and dies out on the range in hot country like this generally is, it starts getting bloated pretty fast." Longarm's voice was still more puzzled than argumentative.

"I know that's the way it is hereabouts," Essie said quickly. "I've see it myself, especially in summertime. A dead steer will bloat real quick when the weather's warm."

Zenia was silent for a moment, and when she spoke her voice was defensive. "Maybe you're both right. But cattle just don't keel over and die for no reason at all. And any other disease except anthrax has other symptoms you can recognize. That's why I'm sure those floating steers died from anthrax and nothing else."

"Oh, I ain't saying you might not be right," Longarm told her hastily. "I was just asking to satisfy my own curiosity."

"Whatever it is that killed those steers, it's got to be stopped before it starts killing Greg's cattle, too," Zenia went on. "I'm just trying to do what I can to help."

"We know that, Zenia," Essie assured her. "And I'm sure Longarm does, too."

"Of course I do," Longarm agreed. "But I never handled a case quite like this one before, so I got to sorta feel my way into it until I get down to something solid." He pushed his chair back from the table and stood up. "Well, I got to do me a little bit of thinking, and I can—" He broke off as the unmistakable creaking of a wagon reached their ears. "It sounds to me like you got company coming up, Essie."

Essie stepped to the window and glanced out. "My lands!" she exclaimed. "It's a spring wagon with a woman and two young men in it. And they've got on funny clothes, all white."

"Oh, my goodness!" Zenia exclaimed. She started toward the window. "That sounds like—" She stopped as she peered over Essie's shoulder. "It is! Well, maybe we'll get to the bottom of this anthrax business now. Come on, Essie. You, too, Longarm. I want you to meet some friends of mine."

"Friends of yours?" Essie said as her sister started for the door. "Zenia Harmon, what kind of stunt have you pulled on me this time?"

"It's not a stunt!" Zenia replied over her shoulder as she started outside. "It's serious business! Come along now."

"Tell me first what's going on!" Essie insisted.

"You'll find out soon enough. I've fixed things up to get you and Greg out of all this trouble, and it just might save your lives as well."

Zenia disappeared through the door. Essie started after her sister and Longarm followed, his curiosity thoroughly aroused. The spring wagon, with a led horse hitched to its tailgate, had halted a few yards from the corner of the house. Two young men wearing white duck suits were in the front seat, one of them holding the reins. Zenia and a young woman who wore a tight-skirted white travelling suit were leaning together beside the vehicle, hugging one another, both talking at the same time.

"Zenia!" Essie said sharply. "What on earth have you done? Who are these people, and what are they doing here?"

Zenia and the woman stopped talking and Zenia turned to face Essie. The woman in the white travelling costume straightened up as she turned, and Longarm's first impression was that she towered over him. Then he saw that, although she was tall, they were about the same height.

Longarm made no effort to mask his stare. The newcomer was indeed tall, but also exceedingly well proportioned. She was also much younger than Zenia, and slim-waisted, with a generous bulge of bosom billowing out the fabric of her jacket. Under the brim of her white straw hat several wisps of blond hair were fluttering in the light breeze. Her cheekbones were high and her chin firm, a firmness strangely at variance with her pertly snubbed nose and wide, generous mouth.

"Essie," Zenia began, then saw Longarm and added, "you, too, Marshal Long. I'd like to introduce my friend Holly Tree. She can introduce her friends. Holly, you've heard me talk a great deal about my sister Essie, and Marshal Long is here to investigate the same case I asked you to come and look into."

Her face showing her bewilderment, Essie said, "Well, I'm always glad to meet one of Zenia's friends, Miss Tree, but I must say you've really taken us by surprise."

"I hope it'll be a pleasant surprise, Mrs. Blanchard," the stranger said. "But it's not Miss, it's Doctor. Dr. Holly Tree, of the United States Army Sanitary Corps. I've come to investigate the anthrax epidemic that Zenia sent me those two telegrams about."

Chapter 9

"Anthrax epidemic!" Essie echoed. "What epidemic are you talking about?"

"Why, the one that's threatening your ranch here!" Holly Tree exclaimed. "The one that Zenia's sent me those two telegrams about this past month."

"Oh, Zenia!" Essie exclaimed. "How on earth could you do such a thing?"

"Because you wouldn't listen to me when I told you how dangerous anthrax is," Zenia retorted. "Sometimes you just exasperate me out of my mind, Essie! You act like I don't know what I'm doing. This time I decided to get somebody here you would have to listen to, somebody who can take charge and do what's got to be done."

"If you have an outbreak of anthrax here, we'll have to get busy at once," Holly Tree broke in. "It's a virulent disease, and very hard to eradicate once it starts spreading."

Longarm decided that he had better take a hand before things went any further. "Miss—That is, Dr. Tree," he began, "Miz Harmon didn't happen to mention it when she sorta introduced us, but I'm a deputy United States marshal outa the Denver office, and I came here to look into some sort of skullduggery that's been going on with cattle, too."

"Good!" Holly said. She nodded toward the wagon, where the two white-uniformed men were watching and listening without trying to disguise their curiosity. "Roger and Burton are the only two aides that could be spared to come with me, and I'm sure we'll need all the help we can get if this is a serious outbreak. We'll have to—"

Longarm interrupted her. "What I'm trying to tell you is that there ain't no outbreak of anthrax here. At least, not as far as I been able to find out."

"Do you have a degree in medicine, or at least in veterinary medicine, as well as being a federal marshal?" Holly asked.

"Of course I don't," Longarm replied.

"Then I can't see that you're qualified to make a judgement on how serious the situation is," she said.

"I don't need no kind of degree to know there ain't no situation!" Longarm protested. "If there was some kind of cattle disease on this ranch, there'd be ailing critters out on the range. If it was something real bad, like anthrax, you'd see carcasses laying around, too. Now, I ain't seen anything like that, and I bet you didn't either, on the way here."

"I'm sure we'll find the signs when we've had time to look," she said. "Now, if you'll excuse me, Marshal Long, we're wasting time talking when I should be getting our facilities ready." Turning away from Longarm, she asked Zenia, "Where would be the best place for us to set up camp?"

"Why . . ." Zenia turned to Essie. "Where do you think, Essie?"

"Back where these folks came from," Essie replied with a tartness Longarm had not see her display before.

"Mrs. Blanchard," Holly Tree broke in, "I can understand how reluctant you and your husband might be to admit you have anthrax-infected cattle on your range. I've seen other ranchers in this same situation before. But I knew your sister's husband quite well when he was with the Sanitary Corps, and I'm sure she learned enough from him to justify her request for us to come here. Why not cooperate with us?"

"Holly's right, Essie," Zenia said quickly. "I know I did the right thing, even if you don't think so."

"I just wish Greg was here!" Essie sighed. "I don't know what in the world he's going to think about all this. Can't we just wait long enough for him to get back before we start thinking about how we can squeeze everybody in?"

"We've been travelling for several days, Mrs. Blanchard," Holly Tree said a bit impatiently. "We need to get started as soon as possible, now that we're here."

Essie suppressed a sigh, then nodded. "I'm sure Greg wouldn't object to your helpers using the barn, and we can move Marshal Long out of there and into the house with us. He can sleep in the kitchen with Frank. Then you could put up with Zenia in her room."

Longarm decided he'd better take a hand. "Maybe Dr. Tree wants to be close by the river, Essie," he suggested. "That way they'd be able to keep an eye out for them floating carcasses a mite easier."

"That sounds very practical," Dr. Tree said a bit stiffly. "It'll probably take several days to make a complete survey of your herd, and I have no intention of leaving until we've done at least that much."

"Well, you're perfectly welcome to stay where you like, I'm sure," Essie said. "But arranging things won't be any trouble, if you don't mind being a little crowded in the house."

"We won't have to disturb you," the doctor assured her. "We have all the equipment we need to set up our own camp, and I'd prefer to be isolated from your place here. But we do need to get started at once."

Longarm turned to Essie again and suggested, "Suppose you let me show 'em someplace along the river. That's where they need to be."

"Yes, the marshal's right," Dr. Tree agreed. "Isn't there a place fairly close by where there's a spring or a stream? I'm not sure I'd want to be drinking out of the Rio Diablo itself, with those carcasses liable to be in it."

"Well, yes," Essie said with a thoughtful frown. "There is." She pointed. "About half or three-quarters of a mile off that way there's the spring where we camped while our house was being built. It's the nicest place I know of close by."

Turning to Dr. Tree, Longarm asked, "Does that sound all right to you?"

"It sounds very good," she nodded. "I'd rather be a little

distance away from the house. There may be times when we'll be testing infectious specimens."

"Ain't that testing job a mite dangerous?"

"Any time you come into contact with a highly infectious disease such as anthrax there's a certain amount of danger. But we wear heavy gutta-percha coated gloves and aprons and take special care not to touch any part of the carcass with our bare hands. That cuts down our risk."

"Just the same, I wouldn't like to be doing it," he said frankly.

"You get used to it, Marshal. We know how to handle the carcasses, but lay people often don't understand the danger in just being close to us when we're working on them. That's why I like to get someplace like where we'll be camping, away from houses and people."

"I'll just get my horse outa the barn, then," Longarm told her. "I ain't unsaddled yet, so I won't be holding you up. If you feel like starting out right away, I'll catch up with you in a jiffy."

Longarm took time in the barn to pick up a hammer from Greg's workbench and set the horseshoe nails in Calceta's loose shoe more firmly than he had been able to do with the rock. Then he swung into the saddle and caught up with the Sanitary Corps wagon before it reached the river.

They had no trouble finding the spot Essie had described. It was easy to see from a distance, for it supported a patch of knee-high brush as well as three struggling trees. A tiny spring had created a patch of taller and greener grass where it bubbled from the ground to form a shallow stream only a foot or so wide. Its bed as it wound the fifty or so yards to join the Rio Diablo was marked by parallel lines of more vividly colored grass than that of the surrounding prairie.

"You figure you and your men will be able to get along all right here, Dr. Tree?" Longarm asked as he dismounted beside the wagon where it had pulled up at the edge of the greenery.

"It'll be just fine, Marshal Long," she nodded. "Now, let me get Moran and Fredericks busy unloading the wagon."

Until now, the two men in the wagon's front seat had made no move to alight. When they heard the doctor mention their names they stood up and dropped to the ground.

"Marshal Long, these are my aides," Holly said. "Roger Moran and Burton Fredericks."

Longarm brought his hand up and started to step forward, but the men saluted him and turned back to Holly Tree.

She went on, "You men go ahead and set up the tent, east of the spring and facing south, I'd say. Put the supplies under that tree over there. The latrine should be downstream a few paces. Get busy now!" She watched the pair as they began working, then turned back to Longarm and said, "While they're getting the camp set up, I'd appreciate it if you'll explain a few things that are bothering me, Marshal."

"Things like why I said there wasn't no anthrax bothering the cattle here?"

"Not so much that. I'll make my own determination about the disease situation. But I need to know the boundaries of this ranch and where the best grazing is found, and most of all, why Zenia Harmon sent those frantic wires to the corps headquarters."

"Well, I ain't been here long enough to be right exact about a lot of things," Longarm began. He paused long enough to take out a cigar and touch a match to it, then went on, "You might say I got pulled into this business through the back door, because it ain't part of my job to worry about what's making cattle sick unless there's some crooked work behind it."

"And you haven't found any?"

"I ain't rightly sure yet. And I sure didn't know anything about them wires you said was sent to the Sanitary Corps."

"We might not have paid any attention to them if they'd been from anyone but Zenia," Holly replied. "But I've known her for a long time. Her husband was my commanding officer when I first joined the corps."

"I sorta figured it might be something like that, after you mentioned getting telegrams. I ain't been here long enough myself to know all the ins and outs, but I was real surprised to hear that Zenia'd sent 'em, and from the way Essie acted, I got the idea Zenia hadn't said anything about 'em."

"Oh, Zenia makes up her own rules as she goes along," Holly said. "I didn't pay much attention to the first one myself. Then I got the second one, and I realized there really must be something wrong here."

"There's something wrong, I grant you that," Longarm nodded. "But I ain't a bit sure it's anthrax."

"Just what do you mean by that?" Holly frowned.

"Well, I ain't had time yet to look for the Blanchards' main

77

herd, and all I've seen is a stray yearling or two, but they've looked mighty healthy to me."

"I've known Zenia for a long time, Marshal Long, and as I just said, she goes about things her own way."

"How'd you come to get acquainted with her?"

"Why, I've already mentioned that Zenia's husband was with the Sanitary Corps for several years before he died."

Nodding, Longarm replied, "So you did. Zenia said something about it, too, but that's all I knew about him till now."

"A few years ago there was an anthrax outbreak in Mexico, just south of the Rio Grande," Holly Tree said. "Mexico was having another of their revolutions, so their government didn't do anything about trying to control it. But they did allow the U.S. to send a Sanitary Corps detachment across the border to keep infected cattle from being shipped into this country. That's where I got acquainted with Zenia and Dr. Harmon."

"Well, that makes everything come clear to me," Longarm said.

Holly went on, "I'm sure Zenia knows how to recognize a case of anthrax, so when I got her telegram I persuaded my commanding officer to let me come here and investigate."

"I wouldn't argue that Zenia might recognize anthrax, Dr. Tree," Longarm said. "Trouble is, she ain't seen a single anthrax-infected critter around here yet, the way I understand things from what Greg Blanchard has told me."

For a moment Holly Tree stood silent, staring at Longarm with disbelief written clearly on her face. At last she said, "Are you positive about that, Marshal?"

His voice turning chilly, Longarm replied, "I ain't got the name of being a liar, Doctor."

"I'm sorry," she said instantly. "I didn't mean to imply you were lying, Marshal Long. I just find it hard to believe that with what she learned from her husband, Zenia would call on the Sanitary Corps for help unless she was sure."

"Mind you now, I ain't questioning that she *thinks* she's right. But somebody thinking a thing's true and it really being true ain't always the same thing. You know, in this job I got I listen to a lot of stories, Dr. Tree, and I have to sorta smell out what's real and what ain't."

"Of course you must," Holly nodded. "Just like a doctor has to sort out what's real and what's imaginary when he listens to a patient trying to explain what's wrong with him." She paused a moment, then went on, "I think I've been underrating you, Marshal Long. We're both after the same thing. Let's be friends as well as working together."

"I'd like that a lot," Longarm nodded.

"We might start out by being less formal," she suggested. "Why don't you forget I'm a doctor and call me Holly?"

"I'll be glad to. And I got a sorta nickname my friends call me that's friendlier than just my name. It's Longarm."

Holly's generous, shapely lips spread in a smile, showing even white teeth. "Of course. The long arm of the law. As you said, it's friendlier than just using your name or title."

"I like it better, anyhow." Longarm pulled out a cigar and flicked his thumbnail across a match to light it. Then he went on, "I didn't get here much before you did, but I've found out a thing or two. Maybe I better tell you about 'em and tell you what got me into this case."

"I've been wondering," Holly confessed. "Since I haven't heard of any crime that's been committed. But why don't we walk along the riverbank while we're talking? We had that wagon shipped from Fort Bliss to Albuquerque, but I've been riding in it now for four long days, and I need to stretch my legs."

As they began strolling upstream beside the Rio Diablo, Longarm told Holly of the suspicion Zenia had passed on to Greg Blanchard that some rancher in the foothills, whose identity was still unknown, had been disposing of the carcasses of anthrax-infected steers by dumping them in the Rio Diablo to float downstream. He did not include his own mishap in tumbling into the Penitente burial cavern, nor did he mention the brief brush he had had with the two riders on his way back to the ranch.

"You don't have any idea where those carcasses that have been floating down the river could have come from?" she asked.

"Not yet, I don't. I was aiming to ride upstream along the Rio Diablo today, but it didn't work out."

"And Zenia thinks those steer carcasses floating downstream are animals killed by anthrax?"

"That's her idea," Longarm nodded. "She figures they drift down to the Canadian. I don't guess you know about the Canadian River, though, not being from around here."

"I've heard of it, of course, but I don't remember hearing anything special about it."

"Well, it's a long, twisted-up river and there's plenty of stretches of quicksand in it on the bottom. Most any of 'em is able to swallow up a steer's carcass."

"But what do you believe, Longarm?" Holly asked.

"I ain't sure yet, and I haven't had time yet to do much noseying around," he confessed. "Something happened to me yesterday that kept me from digging into the case right off, the way I'd planned to. All the same, I ain't right certain them steer carcasses was put in the river just to get rid of 'em."

"What do you think the reason is, then?" Holly asked.

"I'd give a pretty if I could answer that, Holly," he replied. "But when you been on as many cases as I have, with all sorts of crooks doing things that you don't see no real reason for at first, I've learned the smell of rat even when all I get is a tiny little whiff of it."

"And you smell it this time?"

"I sure do. I think your friend Zenia's seeing something that ain't there, and she's so certain she's right that she's got Essie and Greg buffaloed."

"Zenia does have a positive way about her," Holly agreed. "And she holds on to an idea pretty strongly, too."

"How long is it going to take you to find out if there's really anything to this anthrax scare?" he asked.

Holly shook her head. "I wish I could tell you. But until I can get my assistants out scouting around for some carcasses, do a chemical analysis, and study some slides of cattle tissue under a microscope, I haven't any idea."

"Suppose you don't find no carcasses right away?"

"We keep looking until we do." Holly shrugged. "So if you happen to run across one on your way to wherever it is you're going, please take the time to come back and tell me about it."

"I'll sure do that," Longarm promised. "But from what Greg and the others told me, the best chance you'll have of finding one will be in the river."

"Will you be riding along the stream on your way to this place you're going?"

"I reckon I can, easy as not. I'll be glad to keep an eye peeled for any carcasses, if it'll help you any."

"Of course it would, but it just occurred to me that I might as well ride part of the way with you. Roger and Burton will be busy the rest of the day. They'll have to get the camp set up and our testing equipment unpacked and ready."

"Why, I'd be right glad to have your company, Holly. Let's go on back to your camp. I'll help you saddle up, and we'll start out."

Chapter 10

"You know, Holly, it seems to me that if somebody was dumping the carcasses of steers that had died from anthrax in a river, they'd be poisoning the water all the way downstream," Longarm commented. They were riding upstream along the Rio Diablo's bank, their horses side by side, their gait an easy walk.

"It doesn't happen that way, though," she replied. "You know, Longarm, a river's really a living thing. Running water will purify itself as long as there's only a little bit of pollution put in it."

"This one sure looks good and clean," Longarm commented, gesturing to the dancing wavelets of the river.

In the bright midday sunshine the Rio Diablo flowed crystal-clear in its gently winding channel, which was fifty or sixty yards wide here. The water's very clarity made judging its depth difficult, though in a few places the vagaries of the bottom had caused swirls in the current that in turn had created placid pools which Longarm judged would be deep enough to force a horseman to swim his mount across.

At the point they had reached in its upstream course, the river's bottom was sandy for the most part, except for the pools and an occasional rocky shelf over which the stream dashed and which created an area of frothy bubbles which hid the bed. Now and then, even in the places where the bottom was smooth and sandy, the gnarled, water-stripped branches of a mountain cedar from the high slopes of the river's headwaters that had floated down during the spring snowmelt had been caught by some obstruction hidden under the sand to form a snag that trapped bits of debris and created a hazard for an unwary horseman trying to ford the stream.

"It's a nice river," Holly agreed. "But remember that germs are invisible to us, and even clear water like this can be polluted."

"I seen some rivers running through big towns that I'd sure hate to drink out of," Longarm said ruefully.

"Certainly you have. So have I. Streams that have so much polluting material dumped in them that they can't handle it. But a little stream like this one, flowing through country that's not settled yet, wouldn't be polluted by a single steer carcass, even if the animal died from a virulent disease like anthrax."

"Well, that makes me feel a lot better, Holly, even if I still ain't seen no carcasses like the ones Greg Blanchard was telling me about."

"Of course, there'd be an area of polluting right around the carcass," Holly went on. "And if there were a lot of dead infected animals dumped in at once, the stream might not be able to handle them."

"That's one of the things that's been bothering me about this case," Longarm confessed. "When a cattle disease like anthrax hits a herd, it'll generally kill all the critters, not just one or two. Ain't that right?"

"Yes, of course. They won't all die at the same time, and a few of them might even recover. But during that epidemic down in Mexico where I met Zenia and her husband, there were times when a herd of . . . oh, say five hundred head would be wiped out in three or four days."

"Then why ain't Greg and his folks seen more carcasses in the river?" Longarm frowned. "Or out on the range where they're running their herds?"

"It's hard to say. It might be a new strain of anthrax. It might even be a new kind of disease."

"I don't guess you'll know much until you've done some of them tests you was talking about."

Holly shook her head. "No. But from what I've learned since I got here and from what I'm looking at now, I'm beginning to think that Zenia's brought me here on a wild-goose chase. I expected to see a lot of dead steers, but so far I've only seen a few live ones, and all of them have looked healthy."

"Well, I've only been here a day or two longer'n you have, and I sure ain't seen no carcasses, either."

They had reached a sharper bend than was usual in the stream, and the bank ahead had been undercut by the current. Longarm saw the deep shelf running sharply back from the path they'd been following, and turned his horse away from the water's edge, toeing it ahead to take the lead. Holly fell behind him a yard or two.

As he moved forward and the bank levelled out again, he noted casually that the surface of the stream bulged upward in the arc of the bend, as though it flowed over an unusually large boulder. The pronounced hump was the first of its kind that Longarm had seen in the placid stream, and he looked at it with more than casual interest, wondering how such a big boulder happened to be so far from the mountains. Then his eyes adjusted to the glints of sunshine that shifted with the vagaries of the current. He reined in sharply, motioning at the same time for Holly to do the same.

"What is it, Longarm?" she asked. "Is something wrong?"

"I don't know whether it's wrong or right, Holly," he replied as he swung out of his saddle. "But get down here with me where you can see better and tell me if I ain't found what you been looking for."

Holly dismounted quickly and joined Longarm at the edge of the river. She followed his pointing finger and gasped when her vision had adjusted to the shimmer of the current.

"It's a steer carcass!" she exclaimed. "Caught on that big rock." After squinting for a moment through the sheen of sunshine on the river's surface, she went on, "And it looks to me like somebody has tied the carcass to that boulder with a rope of some kind."

"Only it ain't a rope," Longarm said, straightening up from

his stooped position. "It's a tarpaulin that's got all twisted up by the current."

"Are you sure?"

"Certain-sure. And it's likely that carcass has got a slug outa my Winchester in it."

"I don't understand." She frowned.

Longarm filled her in quickly on his brush the day before with the two riders and the burden that was on their led horse.

"I got a pretty good idea I put one shot into that load they had," he concluded. "I didn't get a good close look at it, but I figured it was about the size and shape of a yearling steer." As he spoke, he dropped his hat to the ground, shrugged out of his vest, and began unbuttoning his shirt.

"What're you doing?" Holly asked.

"I aim to swim out there and cut that carcass loose. Then I'll drag it up to the bank, hitch my horse to it, and pull it up where we can get a close look at it. If I find a slug in it, then I won't have to guess about it being the one I got a hunch it is. I'll be sure."

"You can't run the risk of handling that carcass!" Holly protested. "Suppose it's infected?"

"We already talked about that, Holly," Longarm reminded her. "It ain't likely there's a thing wrong with that carcass."

"I can't let you take the risk, Longarm," Holly repeated.

"You sure can't do it yourself," he said. "You'd be running the same risk I would."

"I don't intend to handle it. It's a job for Roger and Burton. They've retrieved enough carcasses to know how careful they have to be. And they've got the gloves and other protective gear that will allow them to handle it safely."

"To tell you the truth, Holly, I'd let them fellows slip plumb outa my mind," Longarm admitted. As much as he hated to back down from doing a job, he saw the wisdom of Holly's words. "All right, Holly. I'll let you do it the way you want to, but I'll expect you to tell me what you find out just as soon as you do all your tests."

"Of course I will!" she agreed. "Now, why don't you go on with what you were starting to do before I took up all your time with my problems. I'll ride back to where we're camped and get Roger and Burton. The sooner we start analyzing that carcass, the better."

"You got any idea how long the job's going to take?"

Holly shook her head. "That's going to depend on how long it takes the boys to set up our laboratory. We might not know anything until this time tomorrow."

At the little livery stable in Valmora, the blacksmith took a close look at Calceta's hoof and nodded. "Eet weel take only a leetle time, *señor*. I make a plug to go where hoof ees tear up, nail new shoe on. Ees not beeg job."

"Good," Longarm said. "I'll just nosey around town while you fix it up and come back after a while."

Valmora might well have been a ghost town for all the activity it displayed, Longarm concluded as he took his first really close look at the hamlet. He'd paid little attention to it when he and Greg had gotten off the train, but now he took the time to observe it carefully. The town straggled up the steep hillside that rose west of the Santa Fe tracks with no semblance of streets or order in the placement of its dwellings. The houses themselves showed no sign of activity. Their doors were closed, their windows had the shades drawn or were blocked by wooden shutters.

Longarm looked down the one short street and found it was deserted, too. The Santa Fe depot beside the tracks was the neatest building the town boasted, though its windows and doors were closed and he saw no signs around it of any activity. There were no pedestrians on the winding dusty street, and the four or five stores along it were empty of customers.

A glance into the small *cantina* showed him that it was also without patrons, but its backbar held a fair assortment of bottles. It looked cool and quiet in the dim interior of the little adobe building, so he pushed the batwings aside and stepped up to the bar.

A grizzled oldster was dozing in a chair tilted up against the back wall. He heard Longarm's boots and opened his eyes, stretched, and came slowly up to the bar.

"*A servicio, amigo,*" he said, his eyes still only half open. "*Que quiere?*" Then, opening his eyes and seeing Longarm clearly for the first time, he went on quickly, "Excuse, please, *señor*. I theenk you are somebody other. You want drink, yes?"

"A tot of rye whiskey, if you got any," Longarm replied.

"Rye whiskey I got. But you tell me sometheeng before I sell you drink. You work for Santa Fe Railroad, no?"

Longarm shook his head. "No. But what's that got to do with selling me a drink?"

"You work for railroad, I don' sell you dreenk! I keek you out my *cantina* and mebbeso I shoot you ass when you go through door!"

"Well, like I just told you, I ain't got nothing to do with the Santa Fe Railroad except to ride on its trains now and again," Longarm said. He dug a cartwheel out of his pocket and spun it on the bar as evidence of his good intentions. "But if you'll bring up a bottle of the best Maryland rye whiskey you got and pour me a drink, I'll be glad to listen to you tell me what the Santa Fe's done that makes you so mad."

The barkeep stepped to the shelves and looked for a moment, then picked up a bottle and placed it on the bar in front of Longarm and added a glass. If the label was to be believed, the bottle held Old Joe Gideon rye, and came from a distillery in Hagerstown. Longarm nodded, shoved the cartwheel to the barkeep, and poured himself a drink.

When he sipped experimentally, he found that the liquor lacked the distinctive smoothness of his favorite Tom Moore, but it had a satisfactory bite and went down well.

"Ees good, no?" the barkeep asked.

"Good enough to drink," Longarm agreed, lighting a cigar.

"I am not see you een Valmora before, no?" The man frowned, and when Longarm shook his head, went on, "I am Pepe Garcia, *señor*. And you?"

"Name's Long. I'm staying down at Blanchard's ranch. Now, go on and tell me what's wrong between you and the Santa Fe."

"Ees not me by myself," the man said. "Ees everybody een Valmora. We espeet on Santa Fe Railroad together."

"You still ain't said why," Longarm pointed out.

"Because ees ruin town!" The barkeep gestured toward the door and went on, "Look outside at estreet! What you see?"

"I looked around before I come in," Longarm told him. He had a reasonably good idea what was coming up. "You got a few stores and houses. That's about all any town in the Territory's got, except maybe Santa Fe and Albuquerque, where there's a lot more people than live here."

"Ees what I am try to say," the man told him. "Was more people here een Valmora unteel Santa Fe ees move shops and all people and build railroad town on line south from here."

To Longarm, as to many others in the West, the complaint was a familiar one. Wherever the expanding railroads established construction railheads when extending their tracks, they either inflated the population of the town nearest the railhead or, in isolated areas where no towns existed, created temporary towns, boomtowns popularly called "Hell On Wheels." The name was well earned, for the construction crews played as hard as they worked, and work generally went on around the clock in two twelve-hour shifts.

"Hell On Wheels" settlements were never thought of as permanent, but moved ahead with the rails. However, in areas where an existing town became construction headquarters, the town boomed suddenly and vastly, then died quickly and drastically when the railroad made its next jump ahead.

Permanent residents of tiny, long-established hamlets which had become boomtowns for three or four or perhaps even as long as six months were usually bitter when the free-spending construction crews moved ahead. Almost invariably, their bitterness increased with time when they saw how the loss of railhead business had deflated the town's population as well as the income its stores and other commercial establishments had enjoyed.

"You can't blame the Santa Fe for moving along," Longarm told the barkeep. "They got a lot of miles to cover before they wind up where they're headed, all the way to California."

"I espeet on them!" the barkeep repeated. "Eef they go a long way, yes, we don' got no right to complain. But ees only so far as five, seex miles. Then they build a town the railroad is own, and call eet Watrous!"

"Is that all the farther it is from here to there?" Longarm frowned. "I figured from the way Greg Blanchard talked that it'd be maybe fifteen or twenty miles."

"You are work for *Señor* Blanchard?"

Longarm shook his head. "No. I just come down here to see if I could give him a hand figuring out a little problem he's run into. Seems like somebody's been throwing cattle carcasses into the Rio Diablo. He's seen 'em floating through his place, and it's got him a mite upset."

"Somebody ees esteal the steers from heem?"

"It don't look that way, but he ain't sure. He says most likely they was rustled from some of the little farms and ranches up in the mountains."

"He ees make good guess, *señor*. From up on slope I have *vecinos*, customers. They esay rustlers ees etake cattle from them."

"Just lately, you mean?"

"*Sí*. Two, maybe three months ago, ees start. Ees still go on, I theenk."

"Your friends up there, don't they brand their steers?"

Pepe shook his head. "Ees nobody een *rio arriba* got so many esteers they need brand, *señor*. They are know each esteer by hees own name."

"You know, Pepe, it don't make no difference whose steers are getting rustled, I'll help get 'em back. If your friends up in the high country tell you anything more about having cattle rustled, you send 'em to see me. I'm staying out at the Blanchard place."

"Eef you are to help *mis amigos* and *Señor* Blanchard, you are welcome to my *cantina*, *Señor* Long," the barkeep said. "He ees not forget hees friends here in Valmora."

"You mean Blanchard still does his trading here instead of going to Watrous?"

"*Sí*," the man replied. "I theenk he does not like the railroad better than anybody else."

Longarm nodded and refilled his glass. He sipped and then asked in a casual tone, "You lived here all your life, I reckon, Pepe?"

"*De verdad, Señor Long*. Ees since a hundred years the first Garcia comes to thees place."

"Maybe you can tell me something I been wondering about."

"What ees eet?"

"A few years ago, I was in this part of the Territory and I heard something about a bunch that calls theirselves Penitentes, some kinda religious outfit. I just got to wondering if there's still some of 'em around."

From the moment Longarm had uttered the word "Penitentes," Pepe Garcia's face had become sober and frozen. He did not reply at once to Longarm's question, but stared across the bar, his expression changing slowly to a frown. "Why you are want to know thees theeng?" he asked at last.

"Just curious, I guess, because I happened to remember what I'd heard about 'em."

"You do not ask me for advice, *Señor* Long, but I weel geeve esome to you. While you are een thees part of Territory, eet ees not wise to be curious about Los Hermanos Penitentes."

"From the way you talk, I take it they're still around?"

"I have esay all I weel esay, *señor*. But seence you are estranger, I tell you again, do not make questions."

There was a finality in Garcia's tone and he underlined what he had just said by digging into his pocket and counting out change for Longarm's dollar, then picking up the bottle of rye and replacing it on the backbar.

Though Longarm would have liked more information, he'd gotten the basic fact he was after about the Penitentes, as well as a bonus in the details of the feud which the townspeople of Valmora were carrying on against the Santa Fe. Picking up his change, he took his time strolling back to the livery stable. The liveryman was just finishing his shoeing job. Still mulling over the way Pepe Garcia had responded to his questions, Longarm mounted and rode out of town, heading south along the railroad right-of-way, headed for Watrous.

Chapter 11

In sharp contrast to Valmora, with its inactivity and its aged and shabby buildings, Watrous was shining new. The usual wide street common to railroad-planned towns had been graded between the town and the tracks. The street started nowhere and went nowhere. Another equally wide street intersected it at right angles to become the new town's main thoroughfare. The depot, freshly painted in the Santa Fe's standard yellow with brown trim, rose on the side of the tracks opposite the town.

New business buildings stood on both sides of the freshly graded street that began beyond the rails. A few of these had been built of adobe, but most of them were of lumber. While many were still unpainted, two or three shone with fresh paint which matched that used on the depot. A short distance from the last of the commercial buildings, the residences began. They were spaced widely apart, and after a few minutes of study,

Longarm realized that between each house enough land had been provided to build another dwelling.

Stores and residences alike, all of the town's structures gleamed, either because they had been freshly painted or because their unpainted sides still had the glistening sheen of recently sawn raw boards which had not yet weathered.

Though Watrous was smaller in area and had fewer houses than many towns which Longarm had seen classed as whistle stops by the Santa Fe, the new depot was the size the railroad usually built only in much larger and better-established towns. Instead of being a compact one-story no-frills structure only large enough to include a waiting room that would accommodate at most a dozen passengers as well as space for a tiny office and baggage room, this depot was two stories high.

A quarter of a mile past the depot, crews were at work building a new roundhouse. Between the roundhouse and the depot, other crews were grading for the network of tracks and shunts and siding that would be required when the roundhouse was placed in operation.

Beyond the business buildings and on the same side of the tracks was a large sidewall tent with a sign in front of it reading OFFICE. An even larger tent stood at a distance on the opposite side of the tracks. It was as big as a small circus tent. Its sides had been drawn up, and Longarm could see rows of tables and in the rear a battery of aproned cooks working over large stoves. Longarm reined his horse toward the smaller tent, eyeing the town beyond the tracks as he rode.

Reaching the tent, Longarm swung out of his saddle and dropped the horse's reins over its head, knowing the animal had been trained to stand. He pushed through the fly of the tent and found himself in a makeshift office. Boards had been butted together to make a crude floor. A line of wooden file cases took up one side of the interior. Some of the file drawers were open, with sheets of paper protruding from them.

On the other side of the tent stood two desks. At one of the desks sat a young man who reminded Longarm very strongly of Billy Vail's pink-cheeked clerk. The other desk was not occupied, but it was piled high with papers in a disarray that somehow managed to appear almost orderly. The youth at the other desk raised his head when Longarm entered.

"If you're looking for a job, you'll have to go find one of the gang foremen and talk to him," the young man said. "Just go back outside and ask any of the workmen. They'll point out their boss to you. I'm sure you'll be hired on. The foremen never seem to have enough men to keep their work up to schedule."

"Thanks kindly for the offer, but I already got a job that suits me right down to a tee," Longarm replied. "What I'm looking for right now is information."

"Information about what?"

"Well, to start off, I'll ask you what your name is. I sorta like to know who I'm talking to."

"My name's Albert Blake." Then, showing more spirit than Longarm had expected, he went on challengingly, "And what's yours?"

"Long. Custis Long. Deputy U.S. marshal outa the Denver office." Longarm took out his wallet and flipped it open to show his badge.

"If you're looking for a wanted man, Marshal, I'm sure you can find several among our work gangs. There are some very ugly-looking men among them."

"It ain't likely the ones I'd want would be hiring themselves out on a job that means hard work," Longarm said. "And anyway, I ain't here looking for fugitives. I just got curious about why the Santa Fe pulled outa Valmora so sudden and moved up here to start a brand-new town."

"You'd have to ask Superintendent Zimmerman about that. I didn't come on the job until the head office had already decided to move the division point here to Watrous."

"And how long ago was that?"

"A little over a month ago."

"So you never worked in Valmora?"

"No. Everything had been moved here and construction was just getting started when I came on the job," the clerk replied.

"And what business is it of this fellow you're talking to when you came to work, Blake?" a man's deep voice spoke from the tent flap.

Longarm wheeled. The speaker was a heavyset, bearded man, almost as broad as he was tall. His cheeks were both high and chubby, making hs eyes look like little slits between them and his thick eyebrows. He had on a corduroy suit and the legs of his trousers were tucked into calf-high laced boots.

"This is U.S. Marshal Long, Mr. Zimmerman," the young clerk said quickly, before Longarm could speak. "He's been asking me questions ever since he came in. I told him he'd have to wait until you got back to get any answers."

"Well, go ahead and ask whatever it is you want to know, Long," Zimmerman said. "But if it involves private Santa Fe business, I might decide not to answer unless you can give me some pretty good reasons why I should."

"Now, I'm not out to pry into anything the Santa Fe might want to keep private, Mr. Zimmerman. This case I'm here on don't have anything to do with railroad business."

"Go on and ask your questions," Zimmerman repeated. "I don't have time to waste in small talk."

"Mainly I'm curious about why the Santa Fe moved outa that little town up north a ways, Valmora."

"Valmora wasn't generating enough freight or passenger traffic to pay for keeping the depot open," Zimmerman replied.

"I don't know all that much about such things, but it'd seem to me that you'd've been better off staying where there was already a town, instead of starting a new one from scratch," Longarm said with a frown.

"You're right when you say you don't know much about such things," Zimmerman said quickly. "New settlers usually favor moving into a new town that's growing instead of an old one that's obviously dying. But that's not the only reason. I guess when you rode up you noticed all the new construction we're doing here?"

"It'd be real hard not to've noticed it."

"That's just the beginning," Zimmerman went on, ignoring Longarm's remark. "A bigger depot, because Watrous will be our new division point and we'll need extra offices. And we wanted enough land to put up a roundhouse and shops and a storage warehouse and side tracks, cattle pens, and loading chutes."

"Seems to me you could've done that where you was and saved some money by not having to start a town, too," Longarm observed.

"You're wrong again. All the land up there is owned by a few families that it was given to on grants when New Mexico was settled by the Spaniards. They wanted more for their land than it was worth."

"When you put it that way, I guess it all makes sense," Longarm said with a nod. "But it seems a shame them people up at Valmora ain't got even a depot any longer."

"Hell, Valmora's only a few miles from here, Long! When the ranchers want to ship, it's not going to hurt 'em to drive their stock the extra distance."

"I guess that's why you don't jump all the way down to Las Vegas? It's a bigger town, but it'd make a lot longer drive for a herd of cattle, I guess."

"Too long," Zimmerman agreed. "But before we're through building, we'll have pens and chutes at Las Vegas, too. That won't be as big a job as the one we're doing here."

"Takes a lot of men to do all that work, I noticed. Mind telling me how many men you got on your payroll?"

"I don't guess that'd do any harm. We're working three hundred men in two shifts."

"Now, that's a right sizeable payroll, but I guess the Santa Fe can afford it," Longarm said. "I seen you got a cook-tent, too, which runs your costs up considerable."

"No, it doesn't. The commissary's contracted outside the company and the men pay for their own meals. We're not soft-headed enough to feed 'em. They'd eat us poor."

Longarm was suddenly aware that he hadn't eaten since breakfast, and that was a long time ago. He said, "You reckon I could get a bite down at that tent? I'll be glad to pay my way, of course."

"Ah, hell, Long! Have a meal on the Santa Fe," Zimmerman said. He raised his voice. "Albert, give the marshal a dinner chip." Turning back to Longarm, he went on, "Now, if I've answered all your questions, I've got work to tend to."

"I've asked myself out for right now," Longarm told him. "If I think of something else, I guess I can find you easy enough."

"I'm not planning on being anywhere but right here," the construction boss said.

He turned and was walking away when the tent flap was raised and a swarthy man with a heavy untrimmed moustache pushed through the opened slit. There was something vaguely familiar about his face, but Longarm couldn't place him as a criminal on the Wanted list he carried in his head.

When the newcomer saw Zimmerman he said, "Oh, there you are. I was looking—"

"We'll talk outside," Zimmerman broke in. "Come on. I'm in a hurry to get down to that switch."

"Switch?" the stranger's voice showed bewilderment.

Zimmerman had reached the tent flap by now. Pushing the new arrival to one side, he took the man's arm and hurried him out of the tent. When Longarm turned back from watching Zimmerman walk away, the young clerk was at his side, holding out a blue disc about the size of a silver dollar.

"Here's your dinner chip, Marshal," he said. "You have to give it to the man who dishes up your meal, or he won't serve you. When you get through eating, leave your plate on the table. One of the dishwashers will pick it up."

"Thanks," Longarm replied, looking curiously at the disc. It reminded him of a poker chip. "I guess these things save you an awful lot of figuring, don't they?"

"They certainly do. The men buy them once a week, when they get paid, and I settle up with the commissary contractor once a week when he turns them in."

"Well, now I got this, I guess I better use it. My belly already thinks my throat's been cut."

As Longarm shouldered through the tent flap and started for the dining tent, he saw Zimmerman and the man who had come to the office. They had stopped at the top of the low grade and were apparently having a heated discussion, for Zimmerman was pounding his fist into the palm of his hand, while his companion shook his head.

Sure as little green apples grows on trees, you seen that fellow someplace before, old son, Longarm told himself silently as he watched the pair. *But if it comes to you and he's wanted someplace, you'll know where he hangs out and you won't have much trouble finding him again. Now, get on about your business, because you got a little bit more riding to do before the day's out.*

Sunset had slipped into dusk and dusk had given way to darkness before Longarm's weary horse mounted the crest of the last low ridge and he saw the lighted windows of the Blanchard ranch house gleaming at the foot of the long slope. Knowing his mount was tired, he resisted the temptation to speed up, and regretted his decision when one by one the windows began going dark. The last light went out while he was still a hundred yards from the house.

He covered the short distance that remained and rounded the corner of the barn. Its doors were open wide enough for him to guide Calceta inside, and he guided the horse through the gap before reining in and swinging out of his saddle.

"I heard hoofbeats when I came out of the house," a woman's voice said from the midnight blackness. "And I knew it must be you getting back, so I thought I'd wait for you and tell you what we found out today."

Longarm had recognized Holly Tree's voice the instant she had started speaking. He said, "I wasn't expecting you to be here."

His eyes adjusted quickly to the gloom of the barn's interior, and he could see the shimmer of Holly's white uniform now. She was standing at the corner of the manger.

"I didn't really plan on being here myself," she replied. "But Roger and Burton worked faster than I'd expected them to."

"What'd they find out?"

"All the preliminary tests were negative," she said. "They still have some cultures brewing, though. We won't be absolutely certain until tomorrow."

"It's still likely to be good news, though, ain't it?"

"Yes, of course. But testing only one animal isn't enough to go by. We'll need to do a lot more before we can be sure."

"So you'll be around a while, yet."

"Quite a while. And I suppose I should've waited until we got a little bit better acquainted instead of—"

"You don't have to play shy with me, Holly," Longarm said. "You're bound to've noticed the way I was admiring you, just like I seen what you was thinking about while we was riding along the riverbank today."

Holly chuckled throatily. "It looks like we're two of a kind, Longarm. I suppose your bedroll's spread up in the loft?"

"Sure. And I'll be up there with you just as soon as I get my horse unsaddled and bedded down."

Longarm made short work of unsaddling and climbed the ladder up to the loft. His eyes were fully adjusted to the darkness by now, and he could see the white patch Holly's uniform made on the straw beside his blanket and the creamy outline of her body against the dark rectangle of the blanket itself.

"You sure ain't one to waste time," he commented as he took off his gunbelt and vest and started levering off his boots.

"I've learned that time's too valuable to waste," she told him. "Do you know what it's like to be one woman on an army base with a lot of young men all around you?"

"Can't say I do, Holly."

"Well, if you know anything about army regulation, you'll know that my name would be mud with a capital M if I even looked like I wanted to have anything to do with an enlisted man. There are times when I feel like a little kid in a candy store, looking at all those goodies in glass jars that she can't open and touch."

"So when you get away from the base, you sorta let go?" Longarm asked, stripping off his trousers and longjohns at the same time. Naked now, he knelt on the edge of the blanket.

Propping herself up on one elbow, Holly leaned forward. Longarm felt the warmth of her breath then the moist caress of her tongue as it traced up and down and around his rigid shaft while Holly sighed deep in her throat.

In their position, there was nothing Longarm could do for Holly except to brace himself with one hand while his free hand wandered over the smooth contours of her big, firm breasts. Holly had his engorged shaft deep in her mouth by now, and her tongue was rasping over it avidly.

Longarm slid his exploring hand down her side and slipped it between her thighs. She jumped and spread her thighs wider to give his hand more room for exploration. He moved his big, hard finger faster, and Holly began wriggling. When her moves grew frantic, she released him and fell back on the blanket.

"Hurry, now!" she gasped. "Get into me quick! I've been without a man so long that I'm about to explode!"

Moving quickly in response to her plea, Longarm positioned himself between her thighs and she guided him into her. Then, as she released her hand, he drove in with a long, fierce thrust that brought a small, involuntary sob from her throat.

"That's it!" she gasped. "Now! Don't make me wait any longer!"

As Longarm started stroking, Holly brought up her legs and locked her ankles behind his back. He increased the tempo of his downward thrusts and Holly responded by rotating her hips as she brought them up in rhythm with his stroking.

Soon she was breathing raggedly, her entire body trembling. Longarm increased the speed of his powerful lunges, and Holly's gasps became small happy screams.

Longarm went in with a full-length lunge and drove home with each long, deliberate stroke that followed. Holly quivered each time he drove into her. Before Longarm had thrust more than a minute or two, she was on the verge of orgasm.

They raced to a climax together, and when Holly shrieked and her hips began bucking Longarm was at the edge of his own climax.

When Longarm at last released her, Holly straightened up and turned to him, holding her head tilted back. Longarm kissed her, and they held their long caress until their tired muscles began to protest.

Holly stepped back. "I'd like nothing better than to start all over again," she said, her upturned face blurred in the darkness. "But I'll be here long enough for us to have other times."

"Sure," he nodded. "And I ain't in no hurry for you to go, but the night's getting on and both of has got work to do tomorrow. And tomorrow night ain't all that far away."

Chapter 12

"So after what you've found out, you're certain-sure there ain't no signs of anthrax on Greg's ranch?" Longarm asked Holly.

"None that I've seen," she replied. "I suppose the best way to put it is that we haven't seen any indication of it."

"I don't reckon that means you've given every steer a close look, of course?"

"Of course not! That would be a ridiculous thing to say. But I went over the area west of the Rio Diablo, and Roger and Burton have covered the eastern range, and they say they haven't run into any infected cattle, either."

Longarm and Holly were lying side by side, stretched out on his bedroll in the hayloft. It was the end of their third night together, and both were too exhausted at the moment to do more than talk. Each time Longarm puffed on his cheroot the glow of its tip outlined their naked bodies shimmering against the dark blankets.

"I ain't seen any sick steers either," he said. "And Greg

says him and the boy has pulled a blank, too. Sounds to me like you was brought up here on a real wild-goose chase."

"I'm afraid you're right, Longarm."

"But I still ain't got the answers to a lot of things I been wondering about," he went on. "Them steer carcasses floating down the river just don't make sense, whatever way I look at it. Who'd want to do a fool thing like that? And why?"

"That's puzzled me, too. The carcass that Roger and Burton pulled out of the river wasn't diseased in any way at all. It did have a rifle slug in its hindquarters, but that certainly wasn't a fatal wound."

"You're right about that, Holly. A shot in the rump don't even slow up a steer," Longarm said. "Anyways, like I told you before, I'd bet a silver cartwheel to a plugged penny that slug came outa my rifle. It's the one I put into it that day when I was trying to stop them two fellows up along the Rio Diablo. They had a carcass lashed on the back of a led horse. Thing is, that don't help you to find out what killed the critter."

"Oh, we didn't have any trouble finding that out. The test for anthrax that Roger and Burton were doing required examining the steer's brain. When they opened the skull to get to the brain they found the steer had been killed just like animals are in a slaughterhouse."

"You mean somebody knocked it in the head with an axe?"

"An axe or a hatchet," Holly replied. "Clubbed it right between the horns."

"Now, that's something else that don't make sense," Longarm said thoughtfully. "But knowing about it might be handy in tying things together for me later on. Of course, it ain't going to make you feel any better, after the long trip you made up here with nothing to show for it."

"I don't have any objections to making the trip," Holly told him. "Because I'd never have met you if Zenia hadn't gotten excited and raised enough of a fuss to have the army send me up here. And I don't need to tell you that I'm unhappy because I don't have an excuse for staying any longer."

"You got to do what your job calls for, the same as I have," he said. "And it ain't as bad as if we'd missed each other completely."

Turning to snuggle up closer to him, Holly said softly, "Even though we've only had a few days together, I'm going to miss you later." Her warm hand slid down Longarm's chest and across the corded muscles of his abdomen to his crotch. Gently squeezing and fondling his shaft, she went on, "It's getting later every minute. Let's don't waste any more time talking."

Longarm walked slowly from the Valmora depot toward Pepe Garcia's *cantina* after the train carrying Holly and her helpers back to Fort Bliss pulled away. He slid a cheroot from his vest pocket and lighted it as he surveyed the dying village. The day was close to its end, but only a few of the houses showed lights in their windows.

Garcia was sitting as he had been when Longarm saw him first, leaning back in a chair propped up against the back wall, his feet dangling. *"Hola, amigo,"* he said, leaning forward, but not far enough to disturb his comfortable position.

"Evening, Pepe," Longarm said. "If you don't feel like getting up, just sit where you are. I know where the bottle I'm looking for is, and I ain't above pouring my own drink."

"Obrigado," Garcia said with a nod. He watched Longarm go to the shelf behind the bar, select the bottle of Old Joe Gideon, and pour himself a generous glassful.

"Maybe I tilted the bottle a mite higher than you would've if you'd been pouring," Longarm said as he settled into the chair next to Pepe's. He held up his glass, filled almost to the brim, and went on, "But that's what you got to look for when you make your customers do the job you oughta be handling."

"Ees worth eet," Garcia replied, a shrug in his voice. "I am not sell enough rye wheeskey to make so much difference."

"Taos Lightning's what you sell the most of, I'd imagine," Longarm suggested.

Garcia straightened up in his chair. "Where you are hear about Taos Lightning, *Señor* Long?"

"Why, this ain't the first case I've had in New Mexico Territory, Pepe. A ways back, I worked a case up in that Taos country, where they got all them little whiskey ranches."

"You are arrest the *paisanos* who make the wheeskey?"

"Nope." Longarm puffed his cheroot until the tip glowed brightly again, then went on, "It ain't my job to collect excise tax, Pepe. You don't have to worry about me butting into your business. I don't give two hoots in hell what kinda liquor you sell. Besides, you've been a real help to me. I sure don't aim to turn you in just because you got a bottle or two of Taos

102

Lightning in your place here."

Garcia nodded, his face showing his relief. "And the *señorita doctora?* She don' find notheeng, so ees go now?"

"Yep. She left on the train just a few minutes ago."

"I am see," the *cantina* owner said. *"Es militaria, no?"*

"Yep. From Fort Bliss, down on the Mexican border."

"You are go esoon, too, maybe?"

"Not till I find out what I came here for."

"But these steers *Señor* Blanchard ees worry about so much, the ones he see float down the Rio Diablo, they do not come from hees *rancho,* no?"

"Now, Pepe, you been here long enough to know the answer to that just like I do. Greg Blanchard don't know within maybe twenty or thirty head exactly how many steers is on his range."

"Es verdad," Garcia agreed.

"I got a pretty good idea them animals was stole up in the hills," Longarm said with a frown. "That puny little Rio Diablo's too shallow to float a carcass till it widens out and gets deeper, a few miles east of Valmora, here." When Garcia nodded agreement, Longarm asked him, "If I recall rightly, when we was talking the other day you said you got a lot of friends that runs cattle up on the high range to the west, where the river starts."

"Seguro," the bar owner replied.

"You heard anything lately from them about cattle turning up missing pretty regular, Pepe?"

"Ees loose a few all time," Garcia said. "Een footheells ees bear, puma, lobo. Up more high ees rough country, steer ees fall over cleeff, een *barranca.* But I hear notheeng more as usual."

"I reckon they'd know right off if they was losing more of their stock than they generally do?"

"Seguro que sí. Ees not beeg ranches een *el altivo.* Feefty, seexty head ees make beeg herd there."

"You'd be sure to hear, if they was losing more'n usual?"

"Een place so leetle like thees one, ees no secret." The bar owner shrugged. "I am know eef ees anytheeng, even esmall theeng, happen een *el altivo."*

"I guess you're right, at that," Longarm agreed. "Liquor has a way of making folks talk more'n they oughta, most of the time." He downed the whiskey that was left in his glass and took a final puff from his cheroot, then stood up and took a cartwheel from his pocket. "I guess I better start looking someplace else now."

Pepe Garcia waved away the dollar Longarm held out and said, "Ees on house thees time. Next time, you have two drinks, pay for them, I am come out even."

"Well, thanks, Pepe," Longarm replied. "I'll drop in next time I'm passing by. And if you hear anything that's connected with what we been talking about, I'd sure like to know."

With another two hours of daylight still remaining, Longarm decided there was no need to hurry back to the Blanchard ranch house. Heading for Watrous, he let his pony pick its own path and set its own pace along the Santa Fe right-of-way as he turned over in his mind the still unresolved aspects of the case.

There ain't none of this makes much sense, old son, he mused as the horse ambled along. *Holly and her crew knocked out the idea that somebody might be trying to hide an anthrax outbreak, and none of the cattle hereabouts shows any signs of hoof-and-mouth disease. So why'd somebody knock down a bunch of steers one at a time and float their carcasses down that fool river?*

Taking out a cigar and lighting it, Longarm mulled the question. With the cheroot lighted and a trail of fragrant tobacco smoke winding in the clear air behind him, he went back to his silent debate.

Now, the Rio Diablo don't start nowhere in particular and it don't go noplace much, except to the Mora River, his thoughts ran. *The Mora goes on to empty into the Canadian, and the Canadian winds down the Texas Panhandle to where it joins with the Red River. Thing is, anyplace a man might look along either one of the two streams the ranchers have more damn cattle than they know what to do with. Another steer carcass don't mean diddledy-squat on them big Texas spreads.*

He kept bouncing the same question back and forth in his mind, trying to dredge up a reason for the floating carcasses, but none occurred to him before he came in sight of the gleaming fresh paint of the new Watrous depot. At this distance, Longarm could see little activity.

There was the usual bustle around the site where the new Santa Fe roundhouse was being built, and the track-laying crews were still wrestling rails into position for shunt tracks and sidings, but the town itself seemed to be slumbering. Only two or three riders and no pedestrians were visible on its newly graded streets, and they were moving slowly.

Following them with his eyes, Longarm was unprepared for the vicious whistle of the rifle slug that cut the air inches from his head, followed by the sharp report of the weapon that had fired it. From the sound of the report, Longarm realized that the unseen ambusher was somewhere ahead and to his right, on the outskirts of Watrous. As he dropped to a half-crouch in his saddle, Longarm flicked his eyes in that direction just as a second slug sang past him. All that he saw was a wisp of powder smoke dissipating in the fitful breeze.

Without wasting time in an effort to locate the exact spot from which the shots had come, Longarm rolled out of the saddle. As he began his defensive move he grabbed the butt of his Winchester and yanked the rifle from its saddle scabbard. He let the weight of his body carry him to the ground.

Dropping flat, the legs of his mount now giving him at least a scanty cover, he scanned the houses in the general area where the wispy muzzle-blast of the second shot had hung for a few fleeting seconds in the quiet late-afternoon air.

Longarm could see now that the would-be bushwhacker had been sheltered by two houses that were only partly completed. They stood some distance apart from the last line of occupied houses that marked the end of the town's main street. Their framework was completed, but no siding had yet been applied to the raw studding and rafters that gleamed yellow in the declining sun.

At the angle from which he was looking, the ends of the two structures overlapped one another. Even though the studs of their walls were bare of siding, the closely spaced upright timbers cast a maze of shadows that provided anyone behind them with a camouflage that was almost as impenetrable to Longarm's eyes as a solid wall.

There's one thing certain-sure, old son, Longarm told himself silently as he examined the shelter. *Whoever triggered them shots off couldn't've been laying for you. There wasn't nobody who knew you was going to be heading this way today, now or at any other time. Which means they just seen you and figured they had a chance of getting rid of you. Which also means that there's still something crooked going on. And that means you still ain't finished the job that brought you here, even if you ain't quite sure yet just what it is.*

Longarm kept his eyes fixed on the framework of the houses. He caught the flicker of movement in the spaces between the vertical timbers of the studding. Distance and the confusing network of shadows cast by the late-afternoon sunshine made it impossible to see clearly what was happening behind the screen concealing his attacker, but he brought his rifle up and snapped off a quick shot at the barely visible target.

"Whoever's behind them houses is certain-sure to make a run for it if he don't get you or you don't get him," Longarm muttered under his breath.

He tried vainly to make out whether his shot had missed or had found a target. The shielding studs that hid the mystery sniper made it impossible for Longarm to see his adversary.

You let him get the jump on you again, he's going to get a start you might not make up, his thoughts ran. *He'd know that rough country north of town a lot better'n you do, and once he gets into them little gullies and ravines he'll be long gone. Best thing you can do, old son, is like old Jeb Hooker said, get there fustest with the mostest.*

Putting his thoughts into action, Longarm scrambled for his horse and swung up, making a high leap that landed him squarely in the saddle. His antagonist must have been thinking along the same lines, for during the split second that Longarm was hanging in mid-air after his high leap, he saw the hidden sniper's horse emerge from cover, its rider bending low over its neck, his heels drumming on the animal's flanks.

Instead of doing what Longarm had expected, trying to escape into the hilly, ravine-cut terrain that lay north of Watrous, the sniper headed for the town.

Longarm had already reined his horse around into a course that would allow him to ride at a long slant after the fleeing bushwhacker before he saw the direction his adversary was taking. Twisting in the saddle, he let off a shot, but the sniper's horse had found its gait in the few seconds that had passed since its rider mounted. Before Longarm could flip the lever of his Winchester and fire again, the fugitive had gained the cover of the nearest houses and disappeared.

Longarm yanked the reins of his horse around and took off at a gallop after the fleeing man. For a moment or two after he began his chase, he thought he had a chance of overtaking the sniper, but the homes of the town were too close. The fugitive reached the first line of dwellings and vanished between two of them. By the time Longarm could reach the point where his quarry had disappeared, the man was nowhere in sight. Reining in, Longarm looked down the street to which his brief chase had led him and shook his head in disgust.

"You come close that time, old son," he muttered as he slid a cheroot out of his pocket. His eyes were still fixed on the street ahead, but he saw no movement. Without relaxing his scrutiny, he took out a match. "Not near enough to win yourself this cigar, but if the first shot that sniping son of a bitch let go had been a little bit lower, you just might not be lighting it right now," he muttered.

Longarm clamped the cigar in his strong teeth and rasped a thumbnail across the match head. A light breeze had started blowing as the day began to die and when the match flared into flame a wind gust caused it to flicker. Longarm cupped his hands together to shield the flame, then bent forward to puff the cigar into life.

His move could not have been better timed. Just as he lowered his head the sharp crack of another rifle shot rang out. The bullet whizzed past Longarm's lowered head and he felt his hat twitch as the slug cut through the edge of its brim. Longarm dug his heels sharply into the flank of his horse. The animal jumped ahead and the sniper's next shot missed.

Longarm had his Colt out now, but he had no target. He reined the horse toward the house from which the mysterious attacker had been firing, his eyes flicking from its half-open door to the single unshuttered window that broke the wall a few feet away from it. The window was partly open, and he could see the fluttering of white curtains stirred by the quickening evening breeze.

He glanced along the street, but saw nobody. When he was within two or three paces of the house he dismounted in a single quick sideways swing and hit the ground running. Three long leaps took him from his horse to the door, which stood ajar.

Longarm hit the door with his shoulder and plunged inside. A quick flick of his eyes showed him that the sparsely furnished room was a combination of living room, dining room, and kitchen. A door on its opposite side, by the wood-burning range, was still swinging gently. The third door, on his right, gaped open and showed the foot of a bedstead. No sound except a small squeaking of hinges from the swinging door broke the silence.

The silence of the house and the slow, declining swinging of its back door told their own story. Longarm stepped to the open bedroom door and swept it with his eyes. It was empty except for a small bureau at one end, the bed at the other end, and a low, armless rocking chair between them.

Longarm went to the back door, pushed it slowly aside, and looked out. The level land on which the town stood stretched for half a mile or so before it was broken by a low ridge. To his right he saw the gleaming rails of the Santa Fe, and beyond them the sloping open range. Whichever way he looked, there was no sign of life or movement.

During the flurry of action that had just ended, Longarm's freshly lighted cheroot had gone out. He puffed, not realizing that the cigar had no coal, and was reaching into his vest pocket for a match to relight it when a woman's voice broke the silence.

"Don't you move a muscle, whoever you are!" she said. "If you do, I'll blow a hole right through you!"

Chapter 13

"Don't worry, I ain't going to do nothing foolish, lady," Longarm replied. He recognized the determination in the woman's voice and stood stock-still, his own voice soft.

"Just move when I tell you to, the way I tell you to," she went on.

"Fine. You call the tune, and I'll sure dance."

"First put your pistol down on the floor," she ordered.

Moving slowly and carefully, he bent forward and deposited the Colt beside his boot toe. As he raised up, he held his hands open, arms spread away from his body.

"Now you can turn around and let me take a look at you," the woman said.

Longarm turned slowly, still holding his arms extended and keeping his hands motionless. He looked into the twin bores of a double-barrelled derringer similar to his own, held firmly and aimed at his chest rather than his head. The woman he faced was young; he judged her to be in her middle or late twenties. She was tall, standing almost as high as Longarm himself, and their eyes met on a level. Hers were bright blue, overlarge, and at first glance gave her face an appearance of innocence.

With a second and closer look the innocence was belied by a long, jagged scar that ran from a corner of her full lips and up her cheek to the outer corner of one eye. The scar was an old one, wealed over now, as pale as the skin surrounding it. Her nose was high-bridged, with flaring nostrils, her cheek-bones prominent, her jaw firmly square.

Longarm could only guess at her figure, for she had on a loose-fitting duck jacket that fell to the middle of her thighs. Below it the billowed folds of a full-cut gingham skirt reached to her ankles. Her hair was caught up in a scarf that covered her head and concealed her ears and browline.

While Longarm was examining the woman, she was treating him to the same sort of scrutiny. He said slowly, keeping his voice at a conversational level, "If you're done looking at me, maybe you'll let me explain why I'm in your house. At least, I reckon it's your house."

"It is. And if you've got any reason at all for being here, I'd certainly like to hear it." Her tone was an echo of Longarm's own, carefully neutral, neither angry nor upset. She seemed to be treating his presence as nothing out of the ordinary, as though it were an everyday occurrence to find a revolver-carrying stranger in her house.

"I guess the first thing I better do is tell you whom I am," Longarm began. "My name's Long, Custis Long. I'm a deputy U. S. marshal outa the Denver office, and I—"

"Wait a minute," she broke in. "If that's true, you'll have a badge or papers of some kind to prove it."

"Oh, I have. If it won't make your finger nervous, I'll be glad to dig out my badge and show it to you."

"Go ahead," she nodded. "Just move slowly."

With his left hand, Longarm dug out his wallet and flipped it open to show his badge. The woman looked at it and nodded, as though she recognized its validity at a glance.

"There's nothing wrong with the badge," she said. "But how am I supposed to know that badge really belongs to you?"

"Well, all I got to offer you for proof is my word, ma'am," Longarm replied. "But if it comes down to that, I ain't got a bit of proof you're who you claim to be, either. For all I know, you haven't got any more business in this house than I have."

For a moment the young woman stared at Longarm, her jaw dropping. Then she smiled and said, "That hadn't occurred to me. But I shouldn't have any trouble convincing you this really is my house, if you have any doubts about it."

Longarm shook his head. "I never did have no reason to think otherwise. You wouldn't be likely to make up something like what you told me. Except I'd sorta like to know your name."

"Elizabeth Whiting. Actually, the house doesn't belong to me, but to my uncle. He owns the general store down by the depot. I work for him, and I'm living here just to keep the place occupied until he can rent it. Then I'll move into a flat he's fixing up for me on the top floor of the store."

"That's as straight an answer as I've ever got," Longarm said with a nod. "And if you ain't convinced yet I'm who I told you, I've met few folks here in Watrous that can tell you who I am. It ain't all that big of a town for you not to know 'em, too."

"Not that I still doubt you, but suppose you give me their names."

"One of 'em's Mr. Zimmerman, the Santa Fe's district superintendent. And there's a young fellow working in the Santa Fe office; his name's Blake."

Nodding, the woman lowered her derringer. "I don't know either of them. I haven't been here long enough to get very well acquainted. But, like you said, it's a small town, and I know their names. All right, Marshal Long. Pick up your gun and tell me what you were doing in my house with a pistol in your hand."

"Why, I was riding in along the railroad right-of-way when somebody begun potshooting at me from that open country past the edge of town," Longarm explained, restoring his Colt to its cross-draw holster. "I took after him and chased him into town a little ways below here. He ducked between houses and I lost sight of him a couple of times. Then, when I got close to him the third time, he ducked inside this house. I followed him as close as I could, but he give me the slip again."

"You followed someone in here?" She frowned.

"Just like I said. I don't reckon you'd have a friend who'd think about using your house while you was away?"

Elizabeth Whiting shook her head, her frown deepening. "I

111

haven't been here long enough to make many friends, Marshal. But I think I might know why the man you were after chose my house. The latch and lock on the front door don't work, and my uncle hasn't had time to replace them. I've got a bolt on the inside, but that doesn't help much when I'm not here."

"Well, that makes it easy to figure out why the fellow I was after picked your house, then. I was getting real close to him, and he just bolted into the first place he found."

"This man you were after . . . is he a bad criminal?"

"I wish I could tell you who he was, but I just plain don't know," Longarm replied. "About the only thing I'm sure of is that he was out to get me."

"I suppose that's one of the risks of your job, isn't it?"

"You could put it that way," Longarm agreed. "But it ain't such a much, when you come down to it." He was suddenly aware that while he'd been talking to the Whiting girl the light had begun to fade. "Now, I better get on about my business. I got a spell of riding to do before I can call it a day."

"Of course," she said. "I imagine the sort of job you have keeps you very busy. But I'm sure we'll run into one another again, in a town as small as Watrous."

"Likely we will," he agreed. "So I'll bid you goodbye now, Miss Whiting. And I hope you ain't spooked by what you run into."

"I don't spook that easily." She smiled. "Until next time, then, Marshal."

Riding toward the Blanchard ranch house, the sky darkening ahead of him, Longarm did a bit of thinking.

You know, old son, you're sorta up shit creek without no paddle on this damned case, he told himself. *About the only thing you're sure of is that something's going on, and you got to find out about it. It ain't going to be easy, not having no more idea than a jackass-rabbit where to begin looking, but if you keep prodding and pushing somebody's bound to get nervous enough to give themselves away, just like that fellow who was taking them potshots at you.*

"So you haven't figured out your next move yet?" Greg Blanchard asked after Longarm had given him a condensed version of what had happened to him during the day.

They were sitting over a final cup of coffee at the supper

table, young Frank listening to their discussion, while Essie and Zenia washed the dishes.

"I gave a little thought to that while I was riding back from Watrous," Longarm replied. "All this has got to be tied in someways to the steer carcasses that you seen floating down the Rio Diablo, but I'm plagued if I can figure out how or why."

"We haven't seen one since Holly's helpers dragged that last carcass out of the river to test it for anthrax." Greg frowned thoughtfully. "Maybe there won't be any more."

Longarm shook his head. "I don't figure that way, Greg," he said. "I'm betting that whoever's been dumping them dead steers in the river just stopped while all the hubbub was going on around your place here."

"And you think they'll start floating downstream again now that Holly and her men have gone?"

"It wouldn't surprise me."

"You'll be watching the river, then?" Greg asked.

"Starting tomorrow," Longarm said. "Things started happening so fast when you and me got here from Denver that I never have had time to cover the whole river. What I aim to do is to ride alongside it from where it flows into the Mora all the way to where it starts flowing across your land."

"It's not a bad ride," Greg said. "The ground doesn't start to hill up until you get close to Valmora, but if I was in your place, I'd do it the other way around. You'll make a little bit better time going downhill than up."

"That hadn't occurred to me," Longarm said. "I'll take your advice, Greg."

"Are you going to be looking for anything special?"

"Mostly just looking. Someplace along the way, I might run onto something that'll be helpful. I guess I can cover it in a day, can't I?"

"It'd be a pretty long day's ride, but I suppose you can do it if you get an early start," Greg told him.

"I'm used to long days in my business," Longarm commented. "I don't suppose another one's going to hurt me much."

Young Frank had been listening to their conversation, looking from his father to Longarm and back to his father again. Now he said, "Dad, I've got all my chores caught up. Please, can I go with Marshal Long and ride the riverbank with him tomorrow?"

Greg hesitated for a moment, then said, "I think you'd better ask him that, Frank. I don't know that he'd want you tagging along, maybe getting in his way."

Before Frank could turn to him, Longarm said, "I'd be right glad to have your company, Frank, if you don't mind getting up before daylight. You know the range a lot better'n I do, so it might be you could show me some things I wouldn't know about otherwise."

Essie and Zenia had been listening while they worked. Now Essie volunteered, "You'll want a lunch to take along tomorrow, Marshal."

"Why, I just figured to ride on in here to the house when we got close to it, and eat with the rest of you," Longarm said. "It ain't more'n a couple of miles, is it?"

"More like three," Greg put in.

"There's no use riding extra miles," Essie went on. "I'll be up early anyhow, because tomorrow's baking day. If you start early enough you ought to get to that little cottonwood grove at the bend by noon. That'd be a nice place to set down and rest while you eat."

"It's all settled then," Longarm said. "And, since we'll be getting away before daylight, I'd say we better not waste no time turning in."

Stars still studded the inky sky when Longarm and Frank set out from the ranch house. A crescent moon hanging at the rim of the horizon provided even less light than the stars.

"It's sort of spooky being out at this time of night, isn't it, Marshal Long?" Frank said after they had covered a mile or so in silence.

"Well, in my business a man gets used to being up and around at all hours," Longarm replied. "The kinda people I'm usually after generally favor working in the dark."

"I guess they do, at that," the youth said thoughtfully. "It must be real exciting to do your kind of work."

"Oh, it ain't such a much, Frank. Mostly it's just looking for men that's turned mean, and they got a way of leaving tracks that you can follow without too much trouble."

"You know, Marshal Long—" Frank began.

Longarm broke in. "I don't usually interrupt somebody, but why don't you just call me Longarm, the way most folks do?"

"You wouldn't mind?"

"I don't see why I should."

"I'd like that, Longarm." Frank's tone of voice hinted at a smile that Longarm couldn't see in the darkness. He went on, "You know, I think I might like to be a lawman myself when I get a little bit older."

"Well, every young fellow's got to make up his mind about what he wants to be, Frank." Longarm was smiling to himself in the shrouding darkness; he'd heard many other youths make the same statement. "You'll do the same, and maybe when you think about it longer it might work out. Or it might not. Whichever way it goes, you got to decide."

They rode on in silence through the darkness. Bit by bit the gloom was replaced by the shimmer that heralded dawn. The stars faded and vanished as the sky slowly grew brighter and details of the land over which they rode became visible. A distant pinpoint of light, then another and still another, showed against the silhouetted western slope.

"That's Valmora waking up, Longarm," Frank said, pointing at the small, brilliant dots. "We're just about at the place where the Rio Diablo flows onto Dad's land."

"This is just about the time I figured we'd get here," Longarm said. "Now all we got to do is ride on down along the bank and keep our eyes peeled to see what we can see."

"What're we really looking for?" the youth asked.

"I'd give a pretty if I knew that myself. I ain't right sure we'll find anything, but I got a real strong hunch that I been missing something by not looking along that little river. And I've learned to play my hunches, because they're generally right."

They reached the river and turned to follow its downstream course. At this stage, just as it flowed from the foothills, the bank sides were regular and the stream was small, twenty to thirty feet across. It was shallow, hock-deep to a horse, thigh-high to a man wading it. The water was a bit roiled; it still carried the silt picked up from the riverbed's hard reddish-ocher soil through which it flowed in coursing down the mountainsides. Its banks were low and level, not straight, but zigzagging in undulating curves through the range grass that grew thick all the way to the water's edge.

As Longarm and Frank continued down the gentler slope

that led to the almost level expanse of rangeland, the stream widened and grew deeper and its current slowed. The water cleared and barely a ripple broke the glassy surface for long stretches. The bottom was plainly visible now, long runs of sand alternating with shelf-rock and occasionally what remained of a long-dead tree, a few snaggy branches rising a foot or so from the bed.

Longarm found little to look at, though his eyes were always busy scanning the stream and the rangeland that now stretched away from it on both sides. He recognized the place where he had forded the Rio Diablo in his first look at the ranch and had wound up in the Penitente burial chamber, but he did not mention the incident to Frank.

They rode slowly, letting their horses set the pace, touching the reins only when one or the other of the animals began veering away from the riverbank. The sun had come up and was climbing its arc in the clear sky when Longarm saw the first signs of disturbed soil at the water's edge. He reined in and Frank pulled up beside him.

"Look ahead there," Longarm told the youth. "Is that a place that your daddy fords regular with a wagon?"

After a quick glance, Frank shook his head. "Not that I know of, Longarm. And I'm real sure I'd know about it if he did."

"You got any idea who'd be hauling something down to the river hereabouts?"

Again Frank shook his head, his face puckering into a puzzled frown. "No, sir. And I'm sure if Dad had noticed them he'd've said something about it."

"Since I been here, I've noticed you folks don't run your herds up this way much. Any reason why?"

"Well, the range is better to the west. And there's the Diablo on one side and the Mora River to the south and Vermijo Creek to the north. They keep the steers sort of corralled, so they don't stray so bad."

"I can see how that'd work," Longarm said with a nod. "Well, let's move along. We still got a ways to go before we're done."

As they continued their steady downstream progress, Longarm saw another spot that stirred his memory. It, too, was marked by wagon-wheel ruts—the place where he and Holly had discovered the snagged steer carcass. Shortly before noon they came to the little stand of trees where the Sanitary Corps trio had set up camp, and stopped to eat lunch.

Here they were almost at the apex of the wide vee in the river's course in which the Blanchard ranch house stood a few miles to the west. They set out after eating and they had ridden only a short distance when Rio Diablo changed its course. As they reached the end of the stream's sharp curve they rode with the sun in their faces.

"It won't bother us long," Frank said, nodding toward the blazing orb as he pulled his hat down so its wide brim would shadow his face. "The river turns south again just a little ways ahead."

"How far are we from the Mora here?" Longarm asked.

"About eight miles. It's pretty level all the way, but we'll be going upslope again when we start home."

"Then we ain't very far from Watrous, are we?"

Frank shook his head. "Not quite ten miles. We'll get closer to it before we hit the Mora, of course."

"Well, we sure ain't seen much that gives us anything to go on," Longarm said, keeping his voice cheerful in spite of the discouragement he was beginning to feel. "I ain't any further ahead than I was when we set out."

"You think you've wasted a day, then?"

"Pretty much so, but I don't begrudge it. I had to take this ride sooner or later, and it's mostly behind me now, so I can start looking other places for the answers I need."

Again they rode in silence while the river changed its course and put the dropping sun at their right. Their horses were beginning to show the effects of the long day they'd had. Now and then they required a prodding toe to keep them moving steadily. The Rio Diablo was deeper here, and wider. As they drew closer to its juncture with the Mora River, the grass receded from the banks and they rode across a steadily widening strip of sand created by swirling currents during the weeks when both streams flowed deeper and faster, swollen by the water rushing down the mountainsides during the summer snowmelt.

"I don't guess we got much farther to go," Longarm observed as their horses slowed, their hooves sinking into the sand. "If we—" He stopped, frowning, then asked, "Do you smell the same thing I do, Frank?"

"I sure do," the youth replied. "And I don't like it."

"No more'n I do," Longarm replied. "Because I've smelled this before, more times than I like to think about. Someplace around here there's something starting to rot. And whatever it is, it's dead."

Chapter 14

"You . . . you mean like a dead body?" Frank asked, his voice a bit shaky.

"Maybe," Longarm nodded. "Why don't you stay here while I take a look around?"

"If you don't mind, I'd rather go with you."

Longarm saw no reason to treat the youth like a child. "Suit yourself," he agreed. "If the smell gets too strong you can always back away."

He toed his horse ahead and moved slowly along the water's edge. After hesitating for a moment, Frank followed him. They had gone only a dozen yards before the stench became almost overpowering. Longarm dismounted, and Frank followed suit.

Longarm stepped to the water's edge, took a bandanna from his hip pocket, and soaked it in the water. The youth did likewise, then followed Longarm's example by folding the bandanna into a triangle and knotting it to cover his nose and mouth. Filtered through the wet fabric, the air was less nau-

119

seating. The two moved slowly along the riverbank until Longarm pointed to a roughly square area of disturbed ground that stretched for twenty or thirty feet a short distance from the streambed.

"That'll be where the smell's coming from," he told Frank, his voice muffled by his improvised mask.

"You think somebody's buried there?"

"Maybe not somebody. But something sure is."

"How're we going to find out? We don't have a spade or anything else to dig with."

"If my hunch is right, we won't need to do much digging. Whatever it is sure ain't buried very deep, or it wouldn't stink things up this way."

They reached the edge of the broken-up ground. Someone had been digging a short distance away from the riverbank, in the area of scoured sand left by the stream's high-water mark. For twenty or thirty square yards around, the sandy soil had obviously been disturbed.

Longarm stepped gingerly onto the broken ground and his boot sank ankle-deep when he put all his weight on it to take a second step. He held his balance by flailing his arms. Then, when he was sure of his footing, he balanced on one foot and began kicking the loose earth aside with the other.

After a dozen or so kicks, the edge of his boot sole struck something hard and glanced off. Longarm swayed for a moment, regained his balance, and started kicking again. He put less force into his effort this time. After a few minutes of kicking, pushing sand aside with his foot, and scraping with his boot toe, his efforts uncovered the head of a steer.

Hunkering down, sickened by the foul stench that filled the air around the head, Longarm examined it quickly. The head had been buried some time ago. The hide covering the head was stretched taut, and the coarse hair was beginning to pull out. The lips had shrunk and pulled away from their normal position. The steer's browned, forward-slanting teeth were fully exposed above a bared strip of white, fleshless jawbone that gave the creature's head the look of a mythical dragon.

As a result of the putrefaction caused by heat and moisture, the animal's eyeballs had burst. When Longarm started to rise to his feet and lift the decomposing head, he almost lost his balance, for the skull seemed to be pulling him down. He looked more closely then at his ugly find and saw that the head was still attached to the hide, which was now stretched from his hands to the point where it disappeared under the area of disturbed soil.

"Looks like we've run into a sorta graveyard," he told Frank, his voice muffled by the tightly drawn bandanna.

"Why would anybody want to bury a dead steer?"

Longarm was studying the surface of the broken ground and did not reply at once. At last he said, "I'd bet a silver cartwheel to a plugged penny there ain't no steers buried here at all."

"But you've got the head of one right there in your hands," Frank protested.

"Sure. Except it ain't attached to nothing but hide. I'd imagine if I pulled out the rest of it, we'd find the critter's hooves on it, and its innards right close by, too."

"Where's the rest of it, then? The meat?"

"Likely cooked up and in somebody's belly. Or was, not too long ago. And if we was able to stand the stink and dig some more, we'd likely uncover a lot more sets of heads and hides and innards."

"Then where did the carcasses go?"

"That's the next thing we're going to have to find out. But the main thing is that now we know what's been happening to them carcasses you folks has seen floating down the Diablo."

"Somebody pulled them to the bank here, and butchered them out?" Frank's young face puckered into a puzzled frown.

"That's bound to be what's been happening, Frank. There ain't no other answer I can see."

"But why, Longarm?"

"That ain't too hard to figure out. But this stink's a mite heavy. Before we go on palavering let's get upwind a ways, where we can catch our breath without gagging."

Longarm dropped the grisly-looking head and walked away. Frank followed him, looking back over his shoulder now and then at the head lying on the riverbank. When Longarm stopped and removed the bandanna, Frank followed his example. Both of them stood looking at the big expanse of torn-up earth while Longarm took out a fresh cigar and lighted it.

"That'll help get that reasty smell outa my windpipe," he said as he puffed out a cloud of smoke. Then he asked Frank, "You figured out yet why somebody'd butcher out a steer carcass?"

"They'd be after the meat, of course. But that's not exactly what I was getting at, Longarm. I meant, why would they want to do the butchering *here?*"

"If you'd stole a steer and was butchering it out, would you like to do it someplace where folks was watching you?"

"I guess not," Frank said. "Because maybe whoever the steer belonged to might see you." His eyes widened with astonishment. "That's why they floated the carcasses down the Rio Diablo, too! They were afraid somebody's see them if they moved them in a wagon or on a packhorse!"

"You hit it right both times," Longarm agreed. "My guess is that they rustled the steers in the mountains up from Valmora. They'd bring the critters down to the river and dump 'em in, and let the current carry them down here."

"How did you figure all that out so quick, Longarm?" Frank asked. "We haven't been here but a few minutes, and you've got it all worked out."

"I reckon I already had all but this last piece in my head, Frank. I guess you remember when me and Dr. Tree run into a steer carcass that'd got snagged upstream? The one they done all the anthrax tests on?"

"Sure," Frank replied.

"Well, I don't know how much talking that bunch from the Sanitary Corps did to you and your folks, but that steer'd been killed just like they do cattle at a stockyard slaughterhouse— knocked between the horns with an axe. Chances are that one laying over there was killed the same way."

"And then whoever killed it just dumped it in the river and let it float down here?"

"Something like that," Longarm said. "But now that we got the stink outa our guzzles, let's just make sure I'm right about what I'm thinking."

Ignoring Frank's puzzled frown, Longarm started circling the area of torn-up earth. Frank hurried to join him, and they had taken only a few steps before Longarm stopped and pointed to the soil. The ruts of wagon wheels and the impressions of mingled hoof- and bootprints showed plainly in the prairie soil. The trail left by the vehicle ran straight west up the sloping prairie.

"That's about what I figured." Longarm nodded. "Whoever's butchering out them steers that's been floating downriver is hauling 'em into Watrous."

"And selling them there?"

"Most likely. The town's outgrowing itself now that the Santa Fe's doing all that work there. How long's it been since you or your daddy came down this way while you was out riding herd?"

"Gee, I don't remember, Longarm. I guess the last time I was along here with my father was maybe two months ago. We don't have much trouble with strays coming down this close to the Mora. I guess you've noticed how thin the grass is along the riverbank, and even a long way back from it."

"It don't look as inviting as it does a ways back to the north," Longarm agreed.

"Dad says it's because the Mora overflows almost every year during snowmelt up in the mountains. It looks like a lake around here for quite a while, and Dad says the water leaches out the soil. Anyway, we generally cut a corner and angle back to the Rio Diablo when we're heading home."

"From the looks of that stretch of dirt past where I pulled out that steer head, there's a lot more heads and hides buried along there," Longarm observed. "And your daddy says you ain't lost much stock lately. So whoever's butchered out them steers didn't get 'em from your herd."

Frank shook his head. "Dad would've noticed if we'd lost a lot of stock. He keeps pretty close track of the cattle."

Longarm squinted at the sky. The sun was hanging low over the peaks that rose west of them. He shook his head and said, "Well, we ain't got time to do much more today. Dark's gonna be setting in by the time we get back to the house, and I need to do some figuring before I push much farther."

Frank gestured toward the exposed steer's skull, which still lay where Longarm had dropped it. "What about that?"

"You mean, am I going to bury it again?"

"That's what I was wondering," the youth said.

"I figure I'll just let it lay like it is, Frank, but I know what you're getting at. If whoever's been butchering here comes to do another job, he's going to see it, all right. And he'll see our bootprints all over the place."

"But suppose he tracks us and comes after you?" Frank asked.

"That's just what I got in mind."

"You *want* him to track you?"

"It'll be a lot easier than for me to try to track him," Longarm said. "He knows the country and I don't."

"But what makes you so sure he'll come looking for you?" Frank insisted.

"I been hunting thieves and robbers and men like that a long time, Frank. I found out quite a few things about 'em. One is that they're always figuring somebody like me is closer to 'em than I really am. So they get nervous and start looking over their shoulder to see how close I am. If they see me, they get jumpier, but if they don't see me they keep on thinking I'm there and get nerved-up just the same."

"You think the man you're looking for is the one who tried to shoot you in Watrous the other day?"

"I'd be surprised if it wasn't him, or one of the men he's in cahoots with. There's got to be three or four tied up in this steer stealing. But one of 'em has got to be the boss, and you can bet that by now he knows who I am and right exactly where to find me. And when he comes calling, I aim to be ready and waiting for him. Now, let's you and me get moving, or we'll be riding in after dark."

"I'm not sure I like this scheme of yours, Longarm," Greg Blanchard said with a frown.

Longarm and Frank had returned to the ranch and told him about the skinning area. Longarm had given a sketchy outline of his plan to the rancher.

"It seems to me you're putting all of us in danger by letting this fellow find you. Suppose he brings along a bunch of his gang, and there's a shootout?" Greg went on.

"He won't be after you folks, Greg," Longarm pointed out. "Before a man like him jumps, he'll be sure of what things are like here on your place. He'll know I'm bunking in the barn."

"Let Longarm do this the way he wants to, Greg," Essie broke in, turning away from the stove. "It's not going to spook me a bit if he tolls those cattle butchers out here so he can arrest them."

"I feel just like Essie does," Zenia added quickly. "Heaven knows, it'll be a relief to all of us to stop being plagued by knowing something outlandish has been going on, but not knowing what it is or why."

"Those fellows he's after could decide to set fire to the house or the barn or both just so they could get at him," Blanchard pointed out.

"I wouldn't put that up as likely," Longarm replied. "This

bunch likes to work quiet, or they wouldn't've set up the kind of scheme they been using."

"I still don't like it."

"You and me and Longarm can all take turns standing watch, Dad," Frank broke in.

"I'll take a turn watching, too," Zenia volunteered.

"So will I, for that matter," Essie added. "It'll be just like it was while we were settling in here, Greg. You remember how we took turns watching out for trouble while we were getting the house built."

"This is men's work, Essie," Greg said sternly. "Three of us can handle a night watch."

"I'll sure do my share," Frank put in eagerly.

"Of course you will, son," Essie said. "All of us will." Turning back to Greg, she went on, "I'd do most anything to get rid of this feeling we've all had that there's something going on we can't figure out."

"Well, even if it was my idea, I didn't stop to figure it might hurt you folks if I tolled them fellows out here," Longarm said quickly. "But it don't make much never-mind where I let 'em look for me. It's all the same to me if I let 'em jump me while I'm riding out on your range by myself, or when I'm going into Valmora or Watrous."

Speaking slowly and thoughtfully, Greg asked Longarm, "It's not likely they'll find out you're hot on their trail for a day or so, is it?"

"It's going to take 'em a while," Longarm agreed.

"Let's just all go about our business, then," the rancher went on. "I can see that your scheme might work, Longarm, and with you and Frank and me splitting up to watch during the night, and Essie and Zenia on the lookout with us during the day, I don't guess they'd be able to surprise us."

"Suppose we try it, then," Longarm suggested. "It ain't likely we'll be bothered tonight. Even if there's a steer floating down the Rio Diablo right now, the bunch that does the skinning out wouldn't go looking for it till daylight."

"Just in case, I'd feel better if we started keeping watch tonight," Greg said. "I'll take it on myself to handle things tonight. We can start splitting the job up tomorrow night."

"I'm not going to have you watch all night by yourself, Greg," Essie said firmly. "Besides, Longarm just told us there's not much chance of any trouble starting right now. I've got some darning I need to catch up on, so I'll just stay up a while. You go to bed and get your rest."

"Call me when you get sleepy, Essie," Zenia told her sister. "I'll watch from whenever you go to bed until Greg and Longarm get up in the morning."

"What about me?" Frank asked.

"You've had a long day riding with Longarm," Essie told the boy. "You sleep, too, son. You'll have your chance to watch tomorrow night."

Longarm woke when the dawnlight grew bright enough to creep into the barn loft. He blinked once or twice, reached for his vest, which lay neatly folded beside his blankets, and fished out the morning's first cigar. As soon as it was drawing well he picked up the bottle of Tom Moore that stood beside the vest and swallowed a quick eye-opener.

A few minutes later he was standing fully dressed beside his bedroll, tipping the bottle of Maryland rye for his pre-breakfast tot, ready to face the day. As he swung off the bottom step of the short ladder that led to the loft, Greg Blanchard came into the barn.

"You were right about last night," the rancher said. "Not a sign of trouble."

"I was sure it'd be that way," Longarm said with a nod. "Them rustlers wouldn't've had time to do much, if they showed up at all at the place me and your boy found yesterday. But today's another thing, Greg. I did a lot of thinking before I went to sleep last night, and I figure I got a pretty good idea of what I better do next."

"Do you want to keep it to yourself, or can you tell me about it?"

"Oh, it ain't all that much of a secret. There's got to be two ends to this rustling business. One's up in the foothills, where the scoundrels pick up their steers from the poor devils who're trying to scratch out a living."

"That'd be the country up north of Valmora?" Greg frowned.

"It's the likeliest place. They'd only be handling one or two steers at a time. You remember how I run into them riders with a packhorse out on your north range, just a day or so after we got here?"

"Of course."

"I figure they was taking a carcass to dump into the Rio

Diablo, to float it down to the place me and Frank found yesterday, where they do their butchering. I'm guessing there's a couple working the Watrous end. They skin out the carcass and take it into the Santa Fe cookhouse and sell it. There's a lot of men working on that railroad job that's got to be fed."

"I hadn't thought about that," Greg said.

"It all hangs together," Longarm went on. "And I don't see as I can get many more answers here."

"You're telling me you're leaving, Longarm?"

Longarm nodded and said, "Looks like I got to, Greg. What I need to do now is nosey around asking a lot of fool questions that nobody in his right mind would come out in the open with."

"Trying to smoke them out?"

"Something like that."

"What can I do to help you?"

"Just sit tight and look after your own affairs."

"It sounds to me like you're just setting yourself up as a target for the rustlers," Greg objected. "Damn it, I got you involved in this, Longarm! I want to help you all I can."

"Now, Greg, it ain't my style to expect somebody else to take on any part of one of my cases. You and your ranch never was wound up in this thing except that they floated them stolen steers down the Rio Diablo and it happens to run through your land. I'm aiming to ride into Valmora after breakfast, and then on down to Watrous. That's where I'll get the answers I need."

Chapter 15

As soon as he finished eating breakfast, Longarm packed his gear and started for Valmora. He kept his horse moving steadily at a good pace and got to the slowly dying hamlet just past noon. As usual, the diminished business section of town on the ridge above the tracks was deserted. The houses that straggled in ragged lines up the steep slope showed only occasional signs of life. He turned his horse toward the *cantina*, dismounted, and went inside.

Pepe Garcia looked as though he had not stirred during the two days that had passed since Longarm's last visit. He was sitting in the chair tilted against the wall, his head leaning back, his *huarache*-shod feet dangling, his eyes closed.

"Hola, amigo," he greeted Longarm. His voice did not have its usual cheerful tone. "You know where to find the bottle you want. But today, put money on the bar before you are have your dreenk. Then you come eseet weeth me and we talk."

"Getting sorta tight-fisted, ain't you, Pepe?" Longarm asked, ignoring the change he sensed in the *cantina* owner's usual cheerful mood.

He tossed a half-dollar on the bar, went behind it to get the bottle of Old Joe Gideon rye, picked it up, and selected a glass from the scanty array on the shelf below. After he had poured his drink, he pulled up a chair beside Garcia and sat down.

"I got the idea you got some trouble you need to talk about, Pepe. You got something wrong with you? The way you're acting, it seems to me you got a bellyache or something."

"Ees not *mi panza*, Longarm. Ees *mi corazon*."

"Heart trouble generally means a woman," Longarm said after he had swallowed a sip of his whiskey. "That what it is?"

"Over women I have no worry. I have *polla*, she ees all I need."

"Then I guess it's just things in general going wrong."

Garcia shook his head. "Last night ees be keel one of *mi compadres*."

"I'm sorry to hear that. Accident of some kind?"

"Murder," the bar owner replied, his voice dropping to a hoarse whisper. "Somebody ees eshoot heem een back."

"Bushwhacked, was he?" Longarm's interest perked up at once. "You got any idea why?" When Garcia shook his head again, Longarm pressed his questioning. "Was it woman trouble? Or somebody that carried a grudge against him? Or was he broke and owed a lot of money to somebody?"

"Thees ees part of worry," the bar owner replied. "I am not know why. He ees have nice wife, everybody like heem. Ees have plenty money, too. He tell me so, two, three month ago."

"Then maybe somebody was after his money, or even his wife," Longarm suggested.

Garcia shook his head again. "Ees nobody I theenk of want to keel heem."

"Well, there ain't no way I know of to change what's happened to him, Pepe. I guess all you can do is get used to it."

"*Creo que sí,*" Garcia agreed, but without losing the sad expression on his face. "Now, I got to go to funeral. Ees make me more sad than before, even." He looked at Longarm with a plea in his eyes and asked, "Mebbeso you go weeth me?"

"I been to way too many funerals, Pepe. I'll beg off going to this one, if you don't mind. Besides, I only come to town today to turn in my horse over at the livery stable. Then I'll be catching the train to Watrous when it comes through."

129

"Ees plenty time," Garcia insisted. "The train eet ees not come for long time. Funeral is last no more as feefteen, twenty minutes."

Without knowing why, Longarm found himself saying, "All right. I guess I'd as lief go with you as to set here by myself. Whenever you're ready, say the word."

Outside, a bell began tolling sonorously. Garcia let the front legs of his chair drop to the floor and stood up. "Ees the time now. *Venga,* Longarm. *Vaminos.*"

"What about my livery horse? I oughta take it back to the stable and turn it in. I'll have to haul my saddlebags and rifle up here and stow 'em in your place while we're gone."

"Put the rifle and *alforjas* eenside. I weel lock door. Nobody ees bother horse, the leetle time we are gone. I weel take heem back to stable."

After Longarm had followed the suggestion and placed his gear in the *cantina,* Garcia led the way up the winding, rock-strewn path to the village. Beyond the casually spaced houses a small stone church with a truncated tin steeple stood half-hidden in the mouth of a little valley cut into one of the precipitous ledges that rose above Valmora.

More than a dozen people were standing around the church, in groups of three or four, engaged in whispered conversations. Most of the women were clad in simple cotton blouses and long voluminous skirts, while the men wore faded cotton jeans and workshirts. A dozen yards away, two saddled horses and a trio of little mountain burros were tethered.

Running his eyes over the groups, Longarm stopped and blinked when he saw Zimmerman. In that small crowd of shabbily dressed residents of the poverty-stricken little village, the Santa Fe's district superintendent stood out like the sorest thumb that could be imagined. He wore a tan corduroy suit, trouser legs tucked into gleaming, highly polished lace-up boots, a white shirt set off by a fancy neckerchief, and a wide-brimmed Stetson.

A moment later, Zimmerman noticed Longarm staring at him. Now it was the Santa Fe man whose jaw dropped in amazement. Longarm did not turn his head away and for a few minutes they both gazed with equal surprise.

Longarm recovered first. He turned his head away, but with the skill of long practice at covert observation kept track of the railroad man's movements with quick, unobtrusive glances. A look or two told him that Zimmerman was working his way to his side, and he was not surprised when the Santa Fe official spoke to him in a half-whisper.

"I didn't expect to see you here, Marshal Long."

"Not any more'n I looked for you to show up, I guess."

"Isn't murder a crime that falls in the jurisdiction of the county sheriff?"

"Sure. But I ain't investigating this murder, Zimmerman. I just come with one of the local men I got acquainted with. He asked me to come along with him, if you're all that interested."

"Curious might be a better word, Marshal. And I noticed you were as surprised to see me as I was to see you."

"Well, you got to admit a man as important as you ain't generally around this kind of funeral."

"I happened to be in Valmora on the orders of my superiors, making an appraisal of the Santa Fe property to report on its possible salvage," Zimmerman explained. "The dead man used to work for the railroad, so I thought it would only be showing common decency if I put in an appearance."

"I see," Longarm said, wondering why Zimmerman thought it necessary to explain his presence. Then he went on, "Not that I was all that curious, but I—"

The tolling of the church bell broke the air and he did not finish his sentence, but said instead, "That's likely to let us know the preaching's about to start. I'd imagine we'll both be catching the train to Watrous, so maybe we can visit a little while then."

Zimmerman nodded and moved away. Longarm joined Pepe Garcia and went into the church. He was surprised at the simplicity and brevity of the service, a short prayer in Latin and an even shorter sermon in Spanish delivered by the priest, who served alone, without even an altar boy. Within a quarter of an hour the roughly clad casket bearers were carrying the coffin to the graveyard behind the church, and most of the people who had attended the service were dispersing.

Longarm followed Pepe Garcia to the graveyard, but stayed a few paces away from the grave itself. Around the edge of the gaping rectangle that had been opened in the hard soil, a small handful of mourners had joined the casket bearers, who were now lowering the unpainted pine box. A fitful wind was blowing, whispering around the corners of the church building. Longarm looked for Zimmerman, but did not see him.

131

Pepe Garcia had followed the coffin all the way to the grave and was standing only a short distance from it. Longarm took out a cigar and flicked a match into flame with his thumbnail. As the match flared up, a gust of wind caught its flame and threatened to extinguish it.

Out of habit, Longarm cupped his hands around the match and bent forward just as a rifle barked from the high ground above. The slug whistled through the air where his head had been only seconds earlier and thunked into the casket with a sound of splintering wood.

Longarm dropped to the ground even before he heard the whine of the bullet and the drumlike reverberation it made when it hit the coffin. Drawing his Colt while he moved, he rolled toward the church. It was the only protection close enough to reach quickly. As he gained his feet behind the church wall, he snapshotted at the spot where he had seen the puff of the rifle's muzzle-blast, but no second shot followed.

Glancing up the slope, he saw a pair of trousered legs and booted feet scrabbling crablike across the bare ground fifty or sixty yards away, in a boulder-sheltered spot where the low-branched *piñon* trees grew thickly. Longarm triggered his Colt again, but the legs of the scuttling rifleman had followed his body and were already out of sight behind the rock outcrop.

Without hesitating, Longarm leaped up and ran around the church to the animals that had been tethered by the mourners. Only one horse and one burro remained. He ran to the horse and freed its reins quickly from the branch of the bushy *piñon* over which they had been looped and vaulted into the saddle. Kicking the horse into motion, he turned its head toward the rocky ledge from which the shot had been fired.

There was no one in sight when Longarm reached the shelf. He reined in, taking fresh cartridges from his pocket and reloading his Colt while he looked and listened. From somewhere ahead he heard a coarse scraping which he recognized at once as being that of a shod horse moving across stones. Twitching the reins, Longarm tried to figure out from which direction the sound of hoofbeats was coming, but in the willywawing wind they could have come from almost anywhere.

There was a trail of sorts, leading upward between small clumps of bushy, low-growing cedars and scattered stands of *piñon* trees. Other than its faint trace, Longarm had no indication what direction the mysterious ambusher might have taken.

It was the only trail uphill, however, and he dug the toe of his boot into the horse's flanks and set out to follow it.

As he gained altitude and moved away from the few scattered houses of Valmora, the size of the *piñon* trees as well as their number increased, and an occasional taller pine appeared among them. The rock ledges occurred less frequently and there were longer stretches of earth rather than stone under the horses' hooves. Longarm could no longer hear the horse ahead of him. He reined his own mount to a slower, quieter pace and began searching the trail for the disturbed patches of soil which would indicate that a rider had passed over it recently.

He rode by a small stone house almost without seeing it, so perfectly did its walls blend in with the niche of the jutting shelf on which it stood. Reining in, Longarm dismounted and walked the few steps to the dwelling. The house could have been a twin to any of the older dwellings Longarm had seen in the vicinity.

It was built of slabs of the layered native stone which everywhere seemed to lie only a few inches below a thin covering of earth. The two- and three-inch-thick slabs had been roughly hewn into strips a foot wide and two to three feet long and arranged in layered tiers, with mud instead of mortar worked into the chinks to get a weatherproof wall. The low-pitched roof, made of wide, overlapped sheets of tin, still appeared intact in spite of the huge areas of heavy rust that coated the metal.

As Longarm drew closer to the isolated structure, he could see that it had been abandoned long ago. There was no front door on the house, but the door opening had been closed with thick boards. The wooden shutter on one of its two front windows was still in place, but the other hung dangling from its twisted bottom hinge, and through it he had a clear view of the bare, deserted interior and windowless side walls. The back wall, like the front, had a center door flanked on each side by windows, and on both back windows as well as the door the wooden closures seemed to be intact.

Satisfied that the man he was chasing had not taken cover in the derelict dwelling, Longarm turned and started back for his horse. He had taken only a step or two, his eyes scanning the thin growth on the ledged slope above him, when the flicker of motion caught his eye.

As had been the case many times in the past, Longarm's

vigilance and keen vision proved to be the margin between death and safety. Without breaking stride he whirled in his tracks, took two giant running strides and dived through the open window as another rifle shot broke the silence. The slug blasted a shower of chips from the cabin's wall.

Longarm landed heavily after his diving leap, but a thick layer of dust on the cabin's earthen floor cushioned his landing. Disregarding the dust, he rolled up to the front wall before rising to his knees. He had slanted his rolling in the direction of the barricaded door, and when he rose to his feet he was sheltered by the strip of thick stone wall between the door and the shuttered window.

For a moment Longarm stood motionless, examining his surroundings. That the cabin had been unused for many years was obvious at first glance. He turned his attention to the closed openings. The timbers sealing the door were nailed tightly together, but lines of light on the shuttered window showed him where there were cracks between the boards, and he stepped over to it. A quick glance located a space wide enough to allow him to peer outside.

Within the limited area that he could scan, nothing moved. The ledge on which the cabin had been built was a thirty- or forty-yard-wide expanse of bare earth and barer stone. The trail up which he had ridden was an old one, and well-marked. The horse he had borrowed so unceremoniously stood unharmed in front of the cabin beside the wide, shallow rut that marked the trail.

"Looks like you sorta got yourself cooped up in a place that ain't going to be as easy to get out of as it was to get into, old son," he told himself aloud. "Unless that damned scoundrel that was sniping at you shows himself, you might just be here for a while."

Sliding a cigar from his vest pocket, Longarm surveyed his involuntary prison. It was barless, but as effective a prison as if it had iron bars so long as the unseen sniper maintained his vigil outside and did not expose himself to a shot. Longarm saw at once that there was absolutely nothing in the bare interior of his shelter that could help him. Only windblown dust lay on the cabin's hard-packed earthen floor.

Well, you was between a rock and a hard place when you jumped in here, Longarm told himself. *And you sure ain't got nothing to help you get outa here with a whole skin, except whatever you can come up with to get rid of that bastard out there. But the first thing you got to do is find out where he's holed up. Once you know that, you can start figuring.*

Applying his eye once again to the slit in the shutter, Longarm watched while the seconds ticked into minutes. He did not break his vigil except to turn away for an instant now and then, long enough to puff at the cigar and keep it lighted. He had smoked it down to a stub before he saw a sign of movement in the low-hanging *piñon* trees on the sloping ground that rose beyond the ledge. Even then, what he saw was a mere twitch of motion, so quick and so faint that he watched the spot for several more minutes before he saw it repeated.

"Whoever he is, he's getting a mite restless," Longarm muttered to himself. "Now, if you give him something to shoot at, he might just take the bait."

For a few more moments, Longarm watched the spot where he had seen the tiny motion, marking it well in his mind. Then he stepped along the wall to the open window beyond the door and stood by it while he planned his next movements.

When he was ready to act, Longarm drew his Colt and took off his hat. Holding the Stetson in his left hand, he extended his arm until a small sliver of the hatbrim extended beyond the windowsill, then drew it back quickly. He bided his time, mentally counting off seconds, until he judged the hidden man would be nerved enough by imagination.

As before, he stretched the hand holding the hat until the edge of the brim was past the window frame, but this time he held it motionless, as though its wearer was anxious to look out, yet hesitant about doing so. Then he pushed his arm forward until the entire brim and part of the crown of the Stetson were framed past the edge of the window.

He had expected the shot from the undergrowth to follow at once, but the sniper delayed for several seconds. Then the rifle barked. Longarm's hat was torn from his hand as a slug cut through it. At the same time, Longarm stepped into the window frame and let off four quick shots that bracketed the spot where a puff of smoke was dissipating in the breeze.

In the area where Longarm had aimed, the rifle spoke again. He heard the clank of metal hitting rock. The slug ricochetted with a screech off the cabin wall outside, well above the win-

135

dow. Longarm held his fire, ready to shoot and move with the slightest stirring of the *piñon* branches, but they were swaying into motionlessness.

Still Longarm did not move. He waited until the foliage was hanging totally still before taking fresh cartridges from his pocket and reloading the Colt. Then he picked up his hat, looked thoughtfully at the bullet holes in it, reshaped it as best he could, and put it on his head.

You needed a new hat anyways, old son, he told himself as he clambered through the window and started walking across the clearing in front of the cabin and up the slope toward the clump of *piñon* trees. *And since it got tore up in line of duty, it'll be paid for by Uncle Sam. I reckon he can stand the ten dollars a good Stetson costs better'n you can.*

Only a few moments were needed to find the sprawled body of the sniper, lying beside his rifle beneath the thick canopy of low-hanging branches. Longarm did not recognize the dead man. He was obviously of Mexican origin, though instead of the cotton jacket and pants and *huaraches* worn by most of the residents of Valmora, he had on covert-cloth trousers, a dark checked flannel shirt, and the high-heeled boots favored by men who rode the range. A high-crowned hat lay beside him, and his horse was tethered a dozen yards away from the trail.

Longarm led the horse to the body and lifted the limp corpse across the saddle. He led the animal back to the deserted house where the mount he had so unceremoniously borrowed stood quietly waiting. Fastening the reins of the dead man's horse to a pair of saddle strings, Longarm swung into his own saddle and started slowly down the trail back toward Valmora.

Chapter 16

Of the group which had attended the funeral, only Pepe Garcia, two other men, and the priest were still at the church when Longarm returned. They stood in front of the door, watching silently as he approached, their eyes not on him, but on the led horse with its somber burden.

Longarm could tell nothing from their faces. All four of them were what in the vernacular of New Mexico Territory had come to be called *"tipo Indio,"* meaning that during the three centuries since the Spaniards conquered New Mexico their original Spanish blood strain had become strongly mixed with that of the natives who had been defeated and subdued but never really tamed by the *conquistadores*.

When Longarm reined in, one of the men who had been standing beside the priest ran toward him. *"Ladron!"* he shouted. *"Es mi caballo! Damele!"*

Longarm knew enough Spanish to understand that he was being called a horse thief, but his command of the language did not extend to a formal reply. He did his best, saying, *"Dispenseme, amigo."*

Pepe Garcia rushed up and took the excited horse owner by the arm. He spoke to him in a low voice, but Longarm could not understand the rapid-fire flow of words between the two. At last the excited *paisano* was calmed, and Pepe turned back to Longarm.

"He ees all right now. I have make heem happy. But you must get off queeck from hees horse. He ees want to go home."

"Can't say I blame him," Longarm said. He swung out of the saddle and handed the reins to the horse's owner, saying, *"Gracias, amigo. Muchas gracias."*

Muttering inaudibly, the horse owner mounted and motioned to the other man who had been standing with him. The second *paisano* leaped on the animal's crupper and the two rode off, the words of their excited conversation soon lost in the distance. The priest had started forward when the altercation began, but had stopped when he saw that Pepe Garcia was taking charge. He stopped beside the remaining horse and stared at the body of its owner.

Pepe inclined his head toward the corpse and asked, "Thees ees the one who shoot at us, no?"

Longarm nodded. "We swapped a few shots up the hill." He took off his hat and held it out to show them the hole torn by the dead man's bullet. "This was the best he could do, and I got in the one that counted. Either one of you know him?"

Pepe and the priest shook their heads. Pepe said, "He is not of our *pais*." Turning to the priest for confirmation, he asked, *"De verdad, padre?"*

His eyes still on the dead man, the priest nodded. Then he looked up at Longarm and said, "And you, my son? Are you of our faith?"

"I'm afraid I'm just another backslider," Longarm replied. "I don't go to no church, Padre."

"But you did not kill this man until he had attacked you?" the priest asked. When Longarm shook his head, he went on, "I will absolve you, then, and pray for his soul as well." Bowing his head, the priest murmured the short ritual phrases in a voice that was barely audible. He crossed himself, looked up to Longarm again, and asked, "Will you see to burying him, or will you leave him with me to be placed in our graveyard?"

"Why, I can't rightly leave him, Padre." Longarm frowned.

"I got to see if I can find out who he is. He was mixed up in this case I'm on, and if I can find out who he ran with, maybe I can finish my business here. I got in mind taking him down to Watrous and seeing if somebody there might not recognize him."

"Very well," the priest replied. "But you will see that he receives a proper burial?"

"Oh, I'll turn his body over to the sheriff or the marshal, or whoever's in charge down there," Longarm said quickly. "He'll get put away decent. You don't need to worry about that."

Pepe Garcia had been growing increasingly impatient during the conversation between Longarm and the priest. He said, "Let us waste no more time, Longarm. You are mees train eef we do not go back queeck."

"I guess you're right about that, Pepe. And I don't cotton to the idea of staying here till tomorrow. Padre, I'll bid you goodbye." Taking the reins of the corpse-laden horse, he went on, "Come along, Pepe. Let's get started."

As they walked down the rocky, slanting path toward the town, Pepe said quietly, "I deed not want to say thees with the *padre* listening. But I have see thees man, Longarm."

"Whereabouts, Pepe? And when?"

"Two, mebbeso three weeks ago. He ees come een *cantina*, have dreenk, talk to nobody, then go."

"And you ain't see him since?"

Garcia shook his head. "I see heem only the one time."

"But you know he ain't from around here?"

"Eef was from Valmora, the *padre* would know heem," the bar owner pointed out.

"Sure. I oughta thought of—" Longarm broke off as the distant whistle of a train cut the late-afternoon air. "You sure were right this time, Pepe. That's the train I oughta be getting on right now, and I ain't got a chance to make it."

"You weel do what, then?"

"Ride on into Watrous, I guess. That livery horse I'm hiring's still down in front of your place. It'll make me late getting there, but I ain't all that rushed for time."

"*Verdad.*" Garcia nodded. "We weell have dreenk, then you go."

●   ●   ●

Dusk was creeping up when Longarm saw the lights of Watrous twinkling faintly against a sky that was just beginning to take on the dark hue which follows sunset. He had taken his time on the ride from Valmora, following the easy grade beside the Santa Fe tracks, letting the livery horse set its own pace while he ran through the unanswered questions of the case that he still had to close.

There ain't nothing much about this case that makes much sense, old son, his thoughts ran. *It's easy to see how Greg Blanchard got all stirred up. That sister-in-law of his just seen ghosts under a bed and roiled up a mess that was nothing but pure imagination. But that's just the icing on the cake, and once it's scraped off, there's still the whole damned cake left to cut.*

Why in tunket would anybody in their right mind go through all that rigmarole about floating steer carcasses down the Rio Diablo from Valmora to have 'em butchered out?

It ain't too hard to figure part of the answer. Them steers was stolen, so whoever rustled 'em didn't dast to pass 'em on to whoever was buying 'em without taking off the hides so nobody'd see the brand.

Except most of them little ranchers up in that Valmora country ain't even got a brand, which is maybe why their cattle is being rustled, because nobody can tell where it come from.

But if that's the case, why would somebody go to the trouble of skinning 'em out before they sell the carcass?

Realizing that his reasoning had done little except carry him around in a circle, Longarm shrugged and rode on into Watrous.

Dusk had merged into darkness by the time he reached the town. A light still showed in both the Santa Fe office tent and the cook-tent, but Longarm passed them by and headed for the main street. He had learned that in new towns which were booming because of railroad construction the marshal's office stood as a sort of buffer between the town and the railroad line.

His guess proved to be correct. A short distance from the tracks he saw the sign "MARSHAL." It was nailed above the door of a board-and-batten building that, in contrast to the structure farther along the street, was unpainted and had a look of being thrown together as a temporary expedient, a building destined for early demolition when a proper town hall was built.

Angling across the street to the hitch rail, Longarm tethered both horses. Beyond the office, where the stores and saloons began, he saw that the streets were crowded even at that early hour. Every second or third place on the main street seemed to be a saloon, and their batwings swung constantly. Roughly dressed men, whom Longarm took to be laborers employed by the Santa Fe on its big expansion job, made up the bulk of the crowd. Longarm had seen his share of boom towns, and the spectacle was not new to him. He pushed into the marshal's office.

"Help you with something, stranger?" asked the man sitting at a paper-piled table in the center of the room. Though full darkness had not yet set in outside, the room was windowless and a lighted coal-oil lamp burned on the table.

"Likely you can," Longarm said. He took in the office with a single quick glance as he spoke. Two barred cells filled its rear half. There was an extra chair at the table and a backless bench along one wall, but otherwise the office was bare. He went on, "Name's Long, Custis Long. Deputy U.S. marshal outa the Denver office."

"Pleas O'Neill, Marshal Long. Glad to make your acquaintance. I've heard your name more than once. Folks call you Longarm, don't they?"

"I answer to it," Longarm nodded. "Looks like you just moved in here."

O'Neal nodded. "I haven't been here much longer than the building. The town council hired me on from down in Lincoln County when the marshal they had took sick and quit."

Longarm had been studying O'Neal's face. He was a young man who looked old in spite of his unwrinkled face and thin, wiry, youthful physique. A hay-yellow moustache swept across his upper lip, its tips waxed to needle points. His chin was short and rounded, his nose aquiline, his brows thin lines that looked like they had been traced with a fine-pointed pen on bulges that protruded finger-thick over their sockets.

"Lincoln County, eh?" Longarm said thoughtfully. "You look a mite too young to've been mixed up in the cattle wars down that way."

"Yes, Billy the Kid was before my time. But I knew most of the ones that survived him."

"Well, I got one outside that didn't survive trying to put me six feet under," Longarm told O'Neal. "And I need a place to keep his body a day or two while I run down the rascals that was in cahoots with him."

"You didn't have your showdown with him in Watrous, Marshal Long, or I'd've heard about it," O'Neal said noncommittally.

"No. Up in Valmora. But it's got some roots here in your town."

"Suppose you tell me about the case."

"Now, I wish I could do that," Longarm said, his voice showing no regret. "But I got good reasons for not talking to nobody about this case till I close it up."

"Men from here are involved in it, I suppose?"

"Likely they are."

"And you don't trust me to keep quiet about it?"

"Now, hold on!" Longarm protested. "If you got a chip on your shoulder, I ain't setting about to knock it off, but that ain't the way of it at all. I just don't talk to nobody about any case I handle till it's closed."

"No offense, Long," O'Neal said quickly. "I'm just trying to find out where I stand. You're accountable to your boss in Denver, but I've got to answer to the officials here who hired me on."

Longarm nodded. "That figures. And seeing you're new on your job, I can't say I blame you for asking questions. But if you don't feel like you can accommodate me, I'll just have to haul that body to your undertaking parlor."

"You'd find the Watrous undertaking parlor's in the back room of Johansen's Furniture Store." O'Neal smiled coldly. "And there's no room for them to keep a body there, any more than there is here in my office."

"You got a couple of empty cells back there that ain't doing a thing but take up space," Longarm pointed out. "And this fellow's fresh dead. He won't smell up your place, at least not for a couple of days."

"Both of those cells back there might be full before the night's out."

"They both got bunks, I see. You could shove the body I need to get rid of underneath a bunk, and it'd be outa the way," Longarm countered.

O'Neal did not reply for a long moment. Then he nodded. "I guess it'll be all right. But just for tonight. You're right about it being quiet in town tonight, but tomorrow's payday for the Santa Fe crew and about this time tomorrow evening I'll more than likely have four or five men in both those cells and be handcuffing the overflow to that bench over there."

"I'll try to be outa your way before you get crowded," Longarm promised. "I'll go drag the body in, then, and get on with my business."

"You'll need a hand, I guess?"

"If you feel inclined. If you don't, I can handle him by myself."

"I'll be glad to help you." O'Neal's voice and manner had changed drastically during the course of this brief conversation. "Bodies are a little unwieldy for one man to handle alone."

"Well, this one ain't had time to stiffen up yet," Longarm remarked as they walked out to the hitch rail.

Night had taken over the sky completely, and little of the illumination from the stores that brightened the street farther up spilled as far as the jail. Longarm and O'Neal lifted the limp body off the horse and carried it into the marshal's office. O'Neal had grasped the dead man's arms, and as they entered the room he glanced down at the frozen face of the corpse. Longarm was sure from the flicker of surprise that passed over his companion's features that he had recognized the dead out-law.

"I see you know who this fellow is," Longarm said quickly.

O'Neal hesitated, as though weighing his answer. "I'm pretty sure I recognize him, but I don't know his name or anything about him. When I first got here about eight months ago, I believe he was on the railroad police force. I can't call his name, though, because I never met him."

"Well, if he's been with the Santa Fe, I ought not have any trouble finding out about him," Longarm said.

"No trouble at all. If I'm right, Mr. Zimmerman or his clerk would be sure to know."

Longarm nodded. "I seen a light out in that big tent they got rigged up for an office. Maybe I'll ride out there and ask 'em soon as I get rid of that extra horse."

"It's not far to the livery stable," O'Neal volunteered. "The next street over and towards town. There's a hotel just across the street from it you'll find comfortable." He gestured toward the cell where the body lay. "I guess you'll be picking him up in the morning sometime?"

"Just as soon as I can," Longarm nodded. "Thanks for the accommodation, O'Neal. Now, if I hyper along I can get my business taken care of and find a restaurant. My belly thinks my throat's been cut, it's been so long since I had a meal."

Leading the horse that had belonged to the dead man, Longarm found the livery stable without trouble and arranged for his own horse to be stalled overnight as well. He checked into the hotel the town marshal had recommended, dropped off his saddlebags and rifle in his room, and started back toward Watrous's main street to look for a restaurant.

As he neared Main Street, he reached into his vest pocket for a stogie. His fingers told him that only one of the long, thin cigars remained between him and a tobaccoless future. The tall, bulky building that housed the general store was on the corner just ahead, and instead of going on to the street he turned at the store's side door and started in. As he was stepping inside, a woman carrying a double armload of packages started out. Longarm could not avoid a collision between them. They brushed together and two of her parcels fell to the floor.

"Well, now, I'm right sorry, ma'am," Longarm said as he stooped to retrieve the fallen bundles. "That was real clumsy of me. I just didn't see you in time to stop."

"No apology's necessary, Marshal Long," she said before he could straighten up.

Surprised to hear her call his name, Longarm stood up and looked at her face. "Miss Whiting, ain't it?" he said, juggling the packages to free a hand so he could doff his hat. "I hope you'll excuse me for being so clumsy."

"It was as much my fault as yours," Elizabeth Whiting said. "I had my mind so set on hurrying home to fix supper that I just didn't see you."

"I hope neither one of them parcels had eggs or something like that in it," Longarm went on, handing her the bundles.

"Nothing breakable," she replied. "I was just trying to carry too much."

"Suppose I give you a hand and help you carry them bundles home," he suggested, deciding his plan to go to the Santa Fe office could be put off a short while. "You do have a pretty good load there."

"Why, I'd appreciate that," she replied. "But I'm sure you had a reason for coming into the store. Go ahead and get what you need. I'll wait for you here by the door."

"All I'm looking for is some cigars," he replied. "It'll only take a minute."

"You'll find the tobacco counter right over there." She

144

pointed. "And, if I remember correctly, those long, thin ones you favor are on the second shelf."

"Then, if you don't mind waiting here, I'll be right back."

With a fresh supply of cheroots in his pocket, Longarm returned and picked up the largest of the bundles Elizabeth Whiting had been carrying. They turned the corner into the main street and started walking toward her house.

"Maybe I shouldn't ask you this," she said as they strolled along the almost deserted street, "but I suppose you've got your case here cleared up by now?"

"I still got some more work to do on it," he replied. "So it looks like I'll be around town for a few days."

"But you're working hard on it, I'm sure."

"Well, it's like this, Miss Whiting." He frowned. "Any case takes a lot of work until you open up some trails to follow. Once you see ahead, you go faster all the time."

"I'd enjoy hearing about your work, Marshal." Elizabeth Whiting hesitated for a moment, then went on, "I was going home to cook my supper, and it's no more work to cook for two than it is for one. Would you stay and eat with me when we get home?"

Duty and pleasure collided in Longarm's mind. He'd had too many invitations from lonely women not to understand that her suggestion meant more than dinner. It was a short struggle, though, and duty won.

"I'd sure like nothing better," he said, "but I got some more business to wind up on my case tonight." A short distance up the street, he saw a café sign, which gave him an idea. He went on, "But I'll tell you what. I got to eat sometime, and I'd a lot rather talk to a pretty lady while I'm eating than to set down by myself. Suppose I take you to supper right now at that restaurant up ahead, and then I'll eat at your house tomorrow evening?"

"That's the best idea I've heard today," she replied. "And I'll accept your invitation. Not only that, I'll promise you a dinner tomorrow evening that no restaurant in Watrous can match."

Chapter 17

Longarm walked along Main Street through the Watrous business section after carrying Elizabeth Whiting's bundles to her house. They had eaten supper, and Longarm felt more cheerful about the world in general. The street was still crowded, though not as much as it had been earlier, and though Watrous boasted no streetlights the lamplight spilling from the doors and windows of the stores and saloons brightened the unpaved thoroughfare.

He reached the corner where the general store stood. Beyond it, the canvas sides of the Santa Fe's office tent still glowed with light, as did those of the cook-tent at the other end of the construction area. Recalling what the town marshal had said about the next day being the railroad's payday, Longarm decided to walk down to the tracks and see if Zimmerman was still at work.

He moved ahead, his eyes adjusting to the darkness as he left the lighted street behind. The flaps of the office tent were closed, but the light was still shining inside. Pushing through the flaps, Longarm saw that Zimmerman's chair between his desk and his work table was vacant, but on the other side of the tent young Albert Blake was still at work, bent over a stack of papers and a large ledger that lay open on his desk. Longarm cleared his throat. Blake jumped with surprise and swivelled around in his chair.

"Oh," he said, relief in his tone. "You startled me, Marshal Long."

"Sorry. I didn't aim to," Longarm apologized. "I didn't come down here to interrupt you, either. I sorta figured that if anybody was working late it'd be Mr. Zimmerman."

"He finished his work and left about half an hour ago. I imagine he's already gone home to bed. I wouldn't be here myself at this time of night, but tomorrow's payday for the construction crews, and I'm just finishing up the payroll figures."

"Well, I didn't mean to break into your work," Longarm told him. "I'll catch hold of Mr. Zimmerman some time tomorrow."

"If it's something I can help you with—"

"Oh, I don't need to bother you while you're so busy."

"All I have left to do is put these ledgers and vouchers in the cabinet, and my job's done."

Blake stood up and closed the ledger, shoved the stack of vouchers into an envelope, and took them to a large cabinet that stood at one side of his desk. He placed them on a shelf, closed and locked the cabinet, and turned back to Longarm.

"I don't think you'd've come here at this time of night if your business wasn't important, Marshal Long," he said. "Now, if there's anything I can do..."

"Well, you just might be able to help me," Longarm told him. "It ain't a very pretty job, though."

"Exactly what is it you need, Marshal?" Blake frowned.

"I got a dead body over in the town lockup that I'm trying to tag a name onto. I understand the dead man used to work for the Santa Fe, and I figured to ask Mr. Zimmerman if he could identify him."

"And since he's not here, you want me to see if I know the dead man?"

"That's the general idea," Longarm nodded.

"I don't know, Marshal Long. Since this construction job

147

started we've had several hundred men on the payroll. A lot of them were drifters who might've worked just a few days before they moved on. I couldn't possibly remember all of them."

"Don't you or Mr. Zimmerman hand out the pay envelopes?"

"Oh, my, no! It would take too much time away from our other work. The foremen come in and pick up the pay envelopes for the men on their work gang."

"How many foremen you got?"

"Twenty-four. Half of them work the early shift, the other half take care of the late shift."

"How come you got two shifts? There's not any night work going on that I've seen."

"No, but it's a sunup to sundown job. The early shift comes on an hour before the late shift and carries the tools and materials to where a gang's working. Then the shift that's come on late stays an hour after the early shift knocks off to clean things up and put the tools away," Blake explained.

"Looks like the foremen are the ones I need to see, all right," Longarm said.

"They'd be able to help you more than I could, or even than Mr. Zimmerman could," Blake agreed.

"I'll come back in the morning, then, when Mr. Zimmerman's here," Longarm said.

"That would be the best thing to do, Marshal Long," Blake agreed. "But I don't know that he's going to be able to give you any more help than I could, because—" He broke off as the tent flap rustled and a man came in.

"Saw your light, Blake, and figured I'd bring down my stuff—" the newcomer began. Then he saw Longarm and went on, "I didn't know you had company. Sorry I butted in."

Longarm looked at the newcomer. He was a stocky man wearing a knit singlet and jeans and a derby hat. His shoulders were broad and his bare arms muscular, but he had a burgeoning pot belly. His face was puffy, with the bulges of scar tissue on his brows, cheekbones, and jaws that marked him to Longarm as either a saloon brawler or an ex-pugilist. He also needed a shave very badly.

"That's all right, Grits," Blake said. "Marshal Long and I were just talking."

"Well, if I ain't busting up anything, I'll give you the tokens and my figures and the money to cover my waybills," the man named Grits said. He tossed a large leather pouch on Blake's desk.

"I'll take care of it," Blake told him. Turning to Longarm, he went on, "This is Grits Veeder, Marshal. It just occurred to me that Grits might be able to identify that body for you. He sees more of the men than either Mr. Zimmerman or I do. He runs the cook-tent."

"What're you talking about, Blake?" Veeder frowned.

"Marshal Long brought in the body of a man who was killed up at Valmora," the clerk explained. "He doesn't know who the man is, but he thinks he used to work here, for the Santa Fe."

"Well, I don't see that I could help him much," Veeder said. "I sure don't know every son of a bitch that ever put in a day's work here. Zimmerman might, but I don't."

"He's the one I come looking for tonight," Longarm told the cook-tent operator. "I'll ask him to take a look at the body first thing in the morning."

"It still wouldn't hurt you any to come along with us and see if you know this dead fellow," Blake insisted. "You see all of them three times a day, every day."

"That don't mean I know every damn one of 'em by name," Veeder retorted.

"You just might remember their faces, even if you don't know their names," Longarm suggested.

"I see so damn many faces going through my chowline that after a while all of 'em look alike," Veeder answered.

"It'd sure be a help if I was even sure this dead man worked on this job here," Longarm went on.

"I'll still beg off, Marshal," Veeder replied. "I see all the dead meat I can stomach while I'm cooking. I sure ain't interested in looking at any more."

"I think it's our duty to help Marshal Long," Blake told Veeder. "Why, if you'll just stop to think about it, if we're not good citizens and help the men that keep law and order, all of us could be in trouble all the time."

"I got plenty of trouble without butting into things that aren't my concern, Blake," Veeder said. "I'll pass."

Longarm had encountered Veeder's type of reaction before, and as always it riled him. He told the cook, "I'd be real obliged if you'd just take a quick look. It might save me a lot of time in getting my case closed up."

"I'll tell you what, Grits," Blake broke in. "I don't think I'd know the dead man either, but I'll go look at him if you'll come along, too."

By now, Longarm's intuition had begun to prod him. He had learned long ago that those who resisted giving him a bit of help in minor matters often had a personal interest in avoiding any kind of contact with those responsible for keeping law and order.

"You know, Veeder," he said, "if I don't get this body identified by tomorrow, I'm going to have to get the Watrous judge to call up a coroner's jury. And anybody that might be able to identify that body can be summonsed to show up and look at it or go to jail if they don't."

"Now, hold on here!" Veeder objected. "The way you put that, it sounds like you're apt to haul me into court if I don't go along with you and Blake."

"Why, I ain't threatening anything," Longarm replied, his voice mild. "But you wouldn't expect me to fall down on my job, and that's what I'd be doing if I didn't ask for a little bit of help from anybody who might be able to help me do my work."

"Let's go with Marshal Long, Grits, and take a look," Blake urged. "If we don't recognize the dead man, all we've got to do is to say so." Turning to Longarm, he asked, "Isn't that right, Marshal Long?"

Longarm nodded.

"Well . . ." Veeder's voice still reflected his reluctance. "Well, I guess I can stand to take a quick look. I'll go along with Blake."

"That sounds a lot better," Longarm said. "Whenever you men are ready, we'll go."

"I'm ready now," Blake volunteered. He stepped over to the desk and blew out the lamp. "I'll be glad to get away from here after such a long day's work."

One side of the tent was in darkness, but the glow from the town's lights filtering through the opposite side gave them enough illumination to pick their way to the flap. In spite of Blake's efforts to start a conversation, Veeder maintained a surly silence as they walked the short distance to the marshal's office. Longarm, preoccupied with his case, answered the young clerk's efforts in monosyllables.

A light burned inside the town marshal's office and the door stood ajar, but there was no sign of Pleas O'Neal. Longarm took the lamp from the table and led his companions back to the cell where he and O'Neal had placed the body. He set the lamp on the floor and turned to Blake and Veeder.

"You men take a look and see if you know him," he said.

Blake dropped to one knee and bent forward, squinting at the corpse's swarthy face. He stared for a moment, frowning, then shook his head.

Getting to his feet, he told Longarm, "I see so many men in the course of my job that I can't be sure, but I don't recall ever seeing this one before."

"How about you?" Longarm asked Veeder.

Veeder knelt and flicked a quick glance at the corpse. "If I ever saw him before, I don't remember him," he said, standing up. "Now, I've taken my look, Marshal. I don't suppose you mind if I go about my business?"

"Not a bit," Longarm replied. "But I was aiming to invite both of you to go along with me to the closest saloon. I'd like to buy you a drink in return for your trouble."

"I don't have time," Veeder said, his voice still surly. "I've got to get some rest, damn it! Three o'clock comes real early in the morning, Marshal, and in case you don't know it, that's when I start to work."

"How about you, Blake?" Longarm asked as Veeder turned and walked toward the door.

"I think I've earned a drink, Marshal Long," the clerk replied. "Not because of looking at that dead man, but because I've done such a lot of extra work today. I'll be right glad to go along with you."

"I noticed a saloon right down the street, next to the general store," Longarm said as they left the building. "It's about the nearest one, so we might as well give it a try."

They walked the short distance to the saloon. The first wave of the evening's customers had flowed past it by now. It was only sparsely patronized, and there was plenty of room for them at the bar.

"Maryland rye," Longarm told the aproned barkeep. "If you got any."

"I'm afraid I haven't got any Maryland, but I've got some real good Pennsylvania rye," the man said. "And some mighty fine bourbon, too, if you'd care to change your mind."

"I'll try the rye," Longarm replied. He tossed a cartwheel on the bar and turned to Blake. "What's your tipple?"

"Oh, I never drink anything stronger than beer," the young man said. "My family back home is Temperance, and they'd be shocked if they knew I was even inside a saloon."

"Well, there's saloons and saloons. Some's bad, some's good," Longarm commented. "I don't see as they've ever hurt me none, and I guess I been in more than my fair share."

By now the bartender had returned. He pushed a foam-capped stein across to Blake, set a shotglass in front of Longarm, and filled it from an ornate bottle.

Longarm sipped the whiskey experimentally and told the man, "It's a mite sweet for my taste, but it'll pass."

He took a handful of coins from his pocket, selected a silver dollar, and tossed it on the bar. The barkeep pulled open the till, scooped up the change, and let it dribble onto the mahogany before sliding the dollar into the till and closing it.

"Oh, my goodness!" Blake exclaimed. "Seeing that money reminded me! I left Veeder's payment on my desk instead of locking it in the safe!"

"I remember him giving you a pouch of some kind," Longarm said with a frown. "But you're right about not locking it up."

"Oh, I know I didn't! And even though we've got a couple of watchmen on night patrol, they wouldn't pay any more attention to the office tent than they generally do."

"You don't think anybody else might go in the tent and see that pouch and know what's in it?"

"Any of the men who eat in the cook-tent could know Veeder puts his money and meal chips in that pouch, Marshal. If one of them should happen to go in the tent . . . Well, I don't have to tell you, we've got some pretty rough fellows out there."

"I seen 'em," Longarm agreed. "From the looks of some of 'em, they've seen the inside of a jail more'n once."

"I'm responsible for that money, Marshal. I've got to go back and lock it up, like I'm supposed to."

"Well, seeing it was partly my fault for busting in on you the way I did, I'll walk back with you, just in case," Longarm volunteered.

"I'd really appreciate it," Blake said, starting away from the bar without finishing his beer.

Longarm downed the remainder of his drink in a swallow and followed him from the bar. Blake set their pace with a fast walk and plunged through the tent flap without looking back to see that Longarm was following. As he crossed the tent to his desk, he struck a match and held it high as it flickered into flame.

When the dancing light showed the pouch lying on the desk just where he had placed it earlier, the young clerk heaved a loud sigh of relief.

"Well, thank goodness!" he exclaimed. "It's still here."

"I figured it oughta be," Longarm said. "But I'm glad nobody got away with it."

"Would you hold the pouch for me, Marshal, while I light another match? I need to be able to see my keys to find the one that fits the cabinet."

Blake extended it to Longarm, who reached for it a split second after the young clerk released it. The bulging pouch dropped to the wooden floor with a thunk. Just before the match flickered and went out, Longarm got a glimpse of meal chips, sheets of paper, and an unsealed envelope which disgorged a thick sheaf of currency as the pouch hit the floor.

"Now, that was certainly clumsy of me!" Blake exclaimed.

"It was my fault more'n it was yours," Longarm said. "Go on and strike another match and light the lamp. It won't take us but a minute to scoop up what fell out."

A match scratched and sputtered as Blake obeyed. This time he got the flame to the lamp wick. Both men looked at the floor. The wide wooden boards were strewn with blue and red and yellow meal chips, sheets of cheap tablet paper scrawled with penciled notations, and the envelope with the thick wad of currency spilling from its flap.

"How come you got three different colors of these meal chips?" Longarm asked as he hunkered down to help Blake scoop up the scattered tokens. "The one you give me the other day was blue, as I recall."

"They're a different color for each meal," Blake replied. "Veeder sets the same price for the three meals every day, but breakfast costs less than the noon meal and supper is the most expensive. It's just to keep things straight."

"Not that it's any of my business," Longarm went on. They had picked up all the chips by now, and he was shuffling the cash together, straightening the bills before putting them into the envelope. "But if the men pay for their meals with chips, how come there's so much cash money here?"

"Oh, that's to take care of the monthly beef waybills."

"I didn't know the Santa Fe was in the beef business."

"It's not. It's just a convenience."

"Now, maybe I don't understand all that much about how some businesses work, but I always thought a waybill was for the freight that a railroad hauls." Longarm frowned. "You said these are beef waybills, and this is one whole hell of a lot of money, unless Veeder gets an awful lot of beef shipped in."

"Well, in Veeder's case, the railroad buys the beef where it's cheapest. To save paperwork, they add what they paid for the beef right onto the waybill."

"And then Veeder pays for the beef and shipping all at the same time?"

"Why, of course. If he didn't, the books wouldn't balance at the end of the month."

"You send the cash on to Chicago, then?"

"Well, I don't. Mr. Zimmerman always goes over my figures just before he mails the ledger sheets, and he puts the money in with them."

"I see," Longarm said. "Well, it ain't none of my business, I reckon. Why don't you just put all this stuff away and we'll head back to town. It's getting late, and I figure it's about time both of us call it a day."

Chapter 18

As the two men walked in the darkness across the strip of unused land between the Santa Fe yards and the town, Longarm went back to the subject of the beef waybills.

"I guess I got my bump of curiosity roused up by them beef shipments we was talking about," he told Blake. "But I never run into a railroad before that does business like the Santa Fe."

"Every road handles its bookkeeping differently, I'm sure," the young clerk said. "Not that I'd be a good judge. The Santa Fe's the only railroad I've ever worked for."

"Meaning no offense, but I got an idea this is the first job you ever had, too," Longarm said.

"As a matter of fact, it is, aside from kids' jobs, the kind I did when I was growing up. I guess I was lucky that Mr. Zimmerman picked me out for it."

"You come all the way out here just hoping you'd get it?"

"Oh, no. Mr. Zimmerman happened to be at the main office

155

in Chicago when I put in my application, and he hired me right then and there."

"I see," Longarm said noncommittally. He paused long enough to light a cigar and went on, "One thing struck me as funny. I didn't see no waybills in that envelope along with the cash."

"No, they're in Mr. Zimmerman's desk," Blake said.

"Instead of giving 'em to you or Veeder, Zimmerman holds on to them, does he?"

"No, not exactly. But I never see them, because when Veeder settles up for the waybills Mr. Zimmerman receipts them and gives them to him. Not that it bothers me, because as Mr. Zimmerman says, I've got enough papers in my desk to keep straight without adding those from the cook-tent."

"I guess he has to work his figures into yours when you start out to balance the books every month?"

"That's right. The Santa Fe pays Veeder for the meal chips and he pays back what they've paid out for beef. It's just a matter of adding up two columns of figures and reconciling the difference between them by subtraction."

"Zimmerman just gives you the figures and you put 'em in the ledgers, is that the way it works out?"

"Of course. I'm sure he's well able to balance a simple set of figures like we have in the beef ledger."

"Maybe I just don't know much about how a business is run, but I still don't see how all this comes out." Longarm frowned. "Now, as I get it, the Santa Fe buys the beef at whatever stockyards it's cheapest, and ships it here on a way-bill. Then Zimmerman collects on the waybills from Veeder and sends the money to the Santa Fe head office, or wherever it is they keep tabs on the deal. Is that right?"

"That's how I understand it." Blake nodded. "But I'll admit it seems confusing the first time you run into it. It got me a little bit mixed up when I first came to work here. That's why Mr. Zimmerman offered to keep on handling the account, because he was familiar with it. But I don't see what connection this has with your case, Marshal Long."

"Neither do I, and it might not have any at all. I guess it just stuck in my mind because of this case I'm on. But it ain't anything for you to worry about."

"If you're still curious, I'm sure Mr. Zimmerman will be glad to explain it to you."

"I'm sure he will, too, son," Longarm said. "And if you don't think it'd get you into trouble, I might ask him about it sometime." They were passing the town marshal's office by now. Lights still glowed inside the building and Longarm inclined his head in its direction as he added, "As soon as we're over the hump of finding out who that dead man laying in there is."

"You'll probably find out tomorrow," Blake said. "Or I guess I ought to've said today, because when I glanced at my watch before we left the yards it was already after midnight. I turn off here at the corner. My rooming house is just off Main Street. So, I'll bid you good night, Marshal Long."

Longarm had not been especially aware of the passing of time until Blake mentioned that midnight was behind them. He looked up Main Street, which was almost deserted, and decided that sleep was more important than a nightcap. Walking down the street to the next corner, he turned and went to his hotel and to bed.

Bright rectangles in the wall of his room opposite the bed were the first things Longarm saw when he opened his eyes. He blinked once or twice, rolled to the edge of the bed, and sat up. His bare feet touching the cool floorboards finished the job of wakening him. He reached for his vest hanging on the back of the chair at his bedside, groped for his watch, and looked at it.

You sure caught up on whatever sleep you missed the past few days, old son, he told himself silently. *Here it is with the morning long gone and you still ain't wide awake.*

Groping in his saddlebags, he pulled out the bottle of Tom Moore that was rolled up in his spare balbriggans and tilted it to his lips. The smooth but fiery rye brought him fully awake and the cheroot he lighted before he began dressing eased the urgent reminders his stomach had been sending him that breakfast was long overdue.

And so is a shave, old son, Longarm told himself as he glanced in the mirror before leaving the room. *You look like something the cat dragged in and couldn't figure out what to do with.*

As he reached the foot of the stairs, his mind on his long-delayed breakfast and a session in a barber's chair, the bald, fragile-looking room clerk behind the desk hailed him as he started toward the door across the lobby.

"Marshal Long! Pleas O'Neal was in here an hour or so ago and left a message for you," the clerk said. "I told him you was up in your room, but he said you'd likely be asleep and he wasn't about to bother you. He said to tell you he'll be in his office if you'd like to stop by."

"Thanks. I'll do that," Longarm replied. "If he comes in again, tell him I'll look in on him soon as I've finished breakfast and got my whiskers scraped off."

An hour later, fed and shaved and redolent of bay rum from the barbershop, his sweeping moustache neatly trimmed, Longarm stepped into the town marshal's office. Pleas O'Neal looked up from the stack of papers that strewed his makeshift desk, reminding Longarm a bit of Billy Vail battling legal paperwork up in Denver.

"I've got some good news," O'Neal said. "I finally found somebody who put a name on that corpse you brought in."

"Well, now, that really is good news. Who in tunket is he?"

"His name's Andres Cruz," the town marshal replied. "Half-breed, Spanish and Jicarilla Apache. Comes from the Rio Arriba country, up above Taos. Had a reputation as a bad one up there, and I guess he brought it right along with him when he came down here."

"You got a lot of information in a mighty short time," Longarm said. "How'd you dig up so much overnight?"

"I'd be lying to you if I said it was anything but luck," O'Neal replied with a thin smile. "I hauled in the usual number of quarrelsome drunks last night, and had to put a few into that cell where we stowed Cruz's body. One of 'em happened to know who he was."

"Well, I'm mighty obliged to you, O'Neal."

"You don't owe me any thanks, Long. Like I said, it was just an accident that I found out."

"At least I got a place to start now," Longarm went on. "I ain't all that interested in Cruz. I'm looking for whoever set him out after me. He sure wasn't just taking it on himself to cut me down up there in Valmora."

"I don't suppose you have any idea who hired him?"

"I wish I did. But hired killers don't go out on their own, so it just stands to reason that somebody paid him."

"There's one more thing you ought to know about Cruz

158

before you have the undertaker come pick him up and bury him," O'Neal said.

"What's that?"

"Before Cruz dropped out of sight here in Watrous, he was working for the Santa Fe," the town marshal replied, his voice flat. "He was one of the guards they hired to watch their yards while the tools and materials for this big construction job were being shipped in."

Longarm sat in silence for a moment, digesting this new bit of information, weaving it into the pattern that he could see forming. He not only saw the pattern taking shape, but saw the holes in it, holes he would have to fill before it was complete.

"Well, that's downright interesting," he told O'Neal. "I owe you. Now I better get on about my case, but first I'll stop by the undertaker's and have him pick up Cruz's body and get it outa your way."

"Take your time, Longarm. He can stay where he is for a while. Just get him off my hands before he starts to smell."

Longarm's visit to the undertaker took only a few minutes. Then he started for the Santa Fe yards. Men were straggling out of the cook-tent back to their jobs. Longarm headed for the office-tent, where he found young Blake at his desk. The larger desk used by Zimmerman was unoccupied.

"I guess your boss ain't finished eating yet?" he said to Blake.

"Why, he's not here, Marshal Long. He rode down to the division office at Las Vegas on the early southbound freight."

"I don't guess he'll be back till tomorrow, then?"

"He said he was going to try to get his business finished there and come back tonight on the northbound mail train. That'd put him in here by about midnight."

"I don't imagine he'll feel much like talking when he gets back. I'll stop by and see him tomorrow."

"Is there something I can help you with?"

"No, thanks, Blake. What I got in mind will wait. Besides, I got a little private business of my own to take care of this evening. I'll catch up with Zimmerman tomorrow."

Leaving the tent, Longarm started walking toward town. He took his time. He still had almost an hour before he was due to meet Elizabeth Whiting for their dinner engagement, and that gave him time to find a saloon where he could get a drink of real Maryland rye.

"I got to admit, that's one of the best dinners I've had in a long time," Longarm said. He took a sip of coffee and reached in his pocket for a cigar, hesitated, then asked, "Would it bother you if I lighted up a cigar, Miss Whiting?"

"Of course not! Go right ahead. And if we're well enough acquainted to have dinner together, we're certainly past the stage where you still need to call me 'Miss Whiting.'"

"Elizabeth, then," he said, flicking his thumb across the head of a match and puffing his cigar until it was drawing well.

"I've got a nickname I like better. Beth."

"Beth, then, if you'd rather. And I got a sorta nickname myself that my friends use."

"Yes, I know. Longarm."

"Where'd you hear that?" he asked.

"From Pleas O'Neal. He was in the store today."

"I didn't know the two of you were even acquainted."

"You know how these small towns are, Longarm. Everybody knows everybody else."

"And usually everything about each other." He smiled.

"Well, I live my own way and I try to keep my life private. Thank goodness, I live out here at the edge of town, and don't have to worry about having any close neighbors looking out their windows, checking up on everything I do."

"Like having me here for supper?"

Beth nodded. "Keeping track of when you got here and when you leave. Or if you leave at all."

"If I knew you a little bit better, Beth, I'd take that as an invitation to stay a while. Maybe quite a while."

"You'd be right, and I'm sure you knew you'd be." She smiled. "What're we waiting for, then?"

"Since you put it to me that way, I don't see that we got to wait at all."

Beth took Longarm's hand and led him into the bedroom. She did not light a lamp, but left the door ajar. The large lamp on the dining table suffused the room with a soft glow. The bedroom was small and the bed large, leaving space for only a small wardrobe chest, a narrow table, and a pair of chairs.

"We're both grownups," Beth said. She was slipping off her dress as she spoke. "There's no reason for us to be coy."

Beth was moving toward him as she spoke. With each step Longarm could see the swaying domes of her breasts under the thin silk of the camisole.

Longarm slipped the straps of her camisole off her softly rounded shoulders. As the silken fabric rippled down and bared her breasts, he bent to kiss their rosy, puckered tips. Beth's body quivered at his touch. With her free hand she began to unbutton his trousers. Longarm's hands were working at the buttons of her knickers. He got the tiny buttons freed at last, spurred by the sensations that Beth's soft hand was creating as she found his burgeoning shaft and cradled it for a moment in her soft palm before closing her hand around it.

"You're as big as I imagined you'd be," she said.

"It's about time for us to get serious," Longarm told her.

"I can't wait any longer!" she gasped.

Longarm started slowly this time, stroking almost gently, lowering himself bit by bit until he'd entered her fully, then holding himself in place firmly. For a while Beth lay quietly, her body only twitching now and then, but as he continued his long, slow strokes without breaking their steady pace, she began writhing and twisting her hips from side to side. After a few minutes Longarm began speeding up his tempo.

Soon Beth began gasping and wriggling, and Longarm speeded up his deep drives. She responded at once and matched his downward thrusts by jerking up her hips to meet him each time he lunged. Longarm sought her lips and she gave him hers, adding to their kiss with a questing tongue.

Longarm began letting himself build now. He bowed his back to give his lusty strokes more force. Beth was well on her way, and she broke their kiss, her head tossing from side to side, her body beginning to quiver. Longarm drove harder and faster, no longer holding himself in check. Beth was crying out softly again and, taking her throaty sighs as a signal, he began his final drive.

"Hurry!" Beth urged. "I'm trying to hold on, but I can't wait much longer!"

With a sudden surge past any that he'd made before, Longarm responded to her plea. Her cries of ecstatic agony were filling the dim room when he reached his limit, but Beth was a minute ahead of him. He drove hard for a few more lusty strokes until his spasm peaked and passed. Beth was already lying exhausted when he gasped in a final sigh of satisfaction and fell forward on her warm, trembling body, spent at last.

For a while they both lay motionless, then Beth broke the silence with a long, satisfied sigh. "I guess I'm greedy," she said. "Nobody's ever made me feel as good before as I do now, but all I can think of is starting all over again."

"It won't hurt us to wait and talk a little while," Longarm told her. "Maybe even doze a bit. But the night's young. It sure ain't over yet, not by a long shot."

Chapter 19

When he felt Beth's first warm, gentle touch on his flaccid shaft, Longarm awakened. He did not move or stir, but lay quiet, keeping his eyes closed. Other women had roused him from sleep in similar fashion, and he'd learned that when he'd reacted too quickly to their soft caresses they'd been disappointed because he'd awakened too soon. He remained motionless while Beth continued to trace the length of his quiescent member with her busy tongue.

Beth kept up her gentle attentions until Longarm was swollen and stiff, then he felt an even greater warmth surrounding his rigid shaft as she engulfed it and began bobbing her head up and down, stopping now and then to hold it shallowly while she explored its satiny tip with her tongue. At last Longarm opened his eyes. Beth was crouched beside him, her own eyes closed as her head slowly rose and fell.

"If you'd like for me to pleasure you the way you're doing

me, you'll have to move a little closer," he said.

Startled, Beth straightened up, releasing him. "How long have you been awake?" she asked.

"Only a minute or two. And I sure felt good when I woke up. Now, if you'd like to go on, move around here where I can reach you and we'll both enjoy ourselves more."

Longarm plunged full length at every stroke, and each time he went home Beth shrieked happily. As he kept up his furious pounding, he felt Beth begin to quiver. The moans that came from her lips turned into small, high-pitched screams. Longarm did not break the tempo of his drives, but kept plunging in, burying his rigid shaft completely with each stroke he sent home.

"Oh, yes!" Beth murmured hoarsely. "This is what I woke up thinking about. Don't stop what you're doing, Longarm! You've got me tingling all over and I love every minute of it!"

Beth moved her hips from side to side, rocked back and forth to increase the pleasure she was getting.

Longarm timed his thrusts to match Beth's moves, which seemed to give her even greater pleasure. She threw back her head and a cry of ecstasy rose from her throat. Her body tossed from side to side, her back arched, and she began to quiver as a series of moans escaped her lips.

Longarm slowed the tempo of his stroking and pressed her close to him. Beth lay motionless for a moment, then looked up and asked, "You're not too tired to go on a few minutes longer, are you? Because this is just the beginning."

"If you'd like it," he replied. "I still got a lot of time to go."

"Oh, that's wonderful." She sighed. "You're the first man I've found so far who can stay with me all the way."

Striding across the open strip between Main Street and the Santa Fe yards, Longarm studied the busy scene the yards presented. Dawn had been breaking when he'd finally left Beth's bed, but he'd had brief periods of sleep. Tired from their explorations of mutual pleasure, they had both needed to nap briefly from time to time between fresh periods of exhausting frenzy. After a brief stop in town for an eye-opener and a hearty breakfast, Longarm now felt almost as good as new, and ready for whatever the day might bring.

Wherever he looked in the broad expanse before him, Longarm saw activity. Track-laying crews were busy putting down rails for sidings, the clank of their spike-sledges ringing through the air. On the far side of the yards, carpenters on scaffolds were applying boards to the skeletal framework of the shops, the sound of their hammering drowned now and then by the ringing of the sledges. There were horse-drawn scoops building up roadbeds, wagons hauling the materials needed by the different crews who were on the job, and everywhere he looked there were a few men who seemed to be scuttling around aimlessly, doing nothing.

Approaching the far edge of the yard from the open range that stretched unbroken to the sweeping rim of the horizon, a wagon with two men on the seat and a tarpaulin-shrouded load caught his eye. He paid little attention to it as it disappeared behind the roundhouse, but when it came into sight again and turned into the yards, he noticed it once more. His interest grew even sharper when the wagon wheeled into the yards and turned to head for the cook-tent.

Longarm watched the vehicle as it rolled to the back of the big tent and disappeared. Then he changed his direction and walked unhurriedly along the edge of the construction area, looking for a spot where he could see the wagon again. He found one beside a gravel pile and stopped to watch just as the wagoneer reined in.

Grits Veeder came out of the tent and walked to the side of the wagon, lifted the tarpaulin, and glanced into the wagonbed. He dropped the canvas and nodded to the men on the seat. They jumped to the ground and talked with Veeder for a few moments before the cook-tent operator went back into the tent. The two men worked briefly at opposite ends of the wagonbed, then lifted out a bulky object shrouded by the tarpaulin. They carried their load into the tent, and Longarm took the opportunity to move closer.

While he was still moving, the men reappeared carrying the tarpaulin. Longarm stopped to avoid attracting their attention, and watched as they repeated their earlier performance with a second load. When they disappeared into the tent this time, Longarm started toward it. He stopped for a moment to look at the wagon, its wheel spokes crusted with moist river sand, then pushed silently through the flap. He drew his Colt as he slipped through the canvas.

165

"I don't give a damn what you found down there at the river!" he heard Veeder say to the wagoneers. "It could've been anybody who dug up that hide. We've got away with this so far without any trouble, and it's making us so damn much money that we'd be fools to get spooked and quit!"

Longarm had heard all that he needed to hear. He stepped the rest of the way through the canvas flap, levelling his Colt as he moved. Veeder was standing with his back to Longarm. He had his pouch in one hand. The other hand was cupped and held a jumble of silver dollars. The men who had come in on the wagon faced the tent opening, but they were so absorbed in their argument with Veeder and with the money in his hand that they did not see Longarm enter until it was too late.

"All of you stand still now, and don't nobody get nervous and go for a gun," Longarm commanded. "You men are right and Veeder is wrong. You're going to quit your little swindle now, whether you want to or not."

"Damn you, Long!" Veeder snapped. "Was it you prowling around over on the Mora?"

"You guessed right," Longarm replied. "And I'll bet a dime to a double eagle that there's enough steer hides and heads buried there to make a pretty good case against you."

"You can't prove anything against me except that I got taken in by a couple of cattle thieves!" Veeder blustered. "These two fellows come to me a while back and offered to sell me butchered-out steers cheaper than I could buy 'em anyplace else. They didn't say where the meat was coming from, and I didn't ask."

"Now, you know that won't hold up in court," Longarm told Veeder. "By the time I put these two men up in front of a judge on a cattle-rustling charge, they'll talk, even if you don't. Why, before the day's out you can just bet they'll tell me who's been doing the actual stealing and dumping the carcasses into the Rio Diablo to float down here, where they haul 'em outa the Diablo at the mouth of the Mora."

"That's still a long way from proving I had anything to do with cattle stealing!" Veeder snapped.

"Oh, I don't imagine I'll have too much trouble proving to a jury that you and your friends have been stealing cattle off the poor little ranchers up in the hills for a long time. I'd say you'll get ten years or better. And that's just for cattle stealing, not for swindling the Santa Fe."

166

"I don't know what you're talking about!" Veeder said, his voice still defiant.

"Well, the law's just about as hard on swindlers as it is on rustlers," Longarm told Veeder. "You been taking money from the Santa Fe under what the law calls false pretenses. I'd say that'll keep you behind bars another five years or so."

"Now, wait a minute, Long," Veeder said. "You can make a lot of money yourself, if you'll just be reasonable."

Longarm knew quite well what was coming next, but to give Veeder still more rope by which to hang himself he asked, "What do you mean by reasonable?"

"Why, there's enough money in this scheme to cut you in for a share," Veeder replied.

"All right, I've heard enough," Longarm snapped. "When I testify that you tried to bribe a federal law officer, that's good enough to keep you in the pen another two or three years."

Ignoring Longarm, Veeder went on, his voice wheedling, "I don't know how much you draw down as a federal marshal, but however much it is, I'll double it if you just forget what you found out. All you've got to do is turn your back and walk away."

Stifling his anger and keeping his voice level, Longarm replied, "I guess you don't hear too good, Veeder. It don't matter a damn *how* big a cut you got in mind. If you knew me at all, you'd know my badge ain't for sale to nobody."

Until now, the two men who had brought in the carcasses had been silent, exchanging glances occasionally. Now one of them spoke. *"Señor, permiteme hablar?"*

Longarm's command of border Spanish was good enough to allow him to understand the question, but he had no intention of letting the wagoneer trick him into using a strange language. He said, "Talk English. I heard enough of what you and Veeder was saying to know you understand it. Now, go on and tell me what's on your mind."

"We are poor *paisanos, señor,*" the wagoneer said. "We are hire to go to Rio Diablo and eskeen dead steers and haul them here. We do not know thees about how somebody ees esteel them. Please, we can go home now?"

"No, you can't," Longarm told the pair. "You'll go to jail, just like Veeder, for handling rustled cattle. If you make a deal to testify against him, I imagine you'll get off light, but I sure don't aim to turn you loose."

"But, *señor*—"

"That's enough," Longarm said.

He motioned with the barrel of the Colt for the wagoneers to stand back. Reaching under his coat with his left hand, he took his handcuffs from his belt. The cuffs were snapped closed and he hung them over his right wrist while reaching into his vest pocket for the key. Working the tiny key with his left hand was a bit awkward, but after a moment of fumbling he got them open. Returning the key to his pocket, he took the cuffs and stepped up to the cook-tent operator.

"I only got one pair of cuffs, so you'll be the one to wear 'em, Veeder. I don't look for no trouble from these two while I'm marching all of you to jail, but I ain't so sure about you."

"Think again about that offer I made you, Long," Veeder urged as Longarm stepped up to him with the cuffs. "You can make a lot more money working with me than you can by putting me in prison."

"I already told you, I ain't for sale," Longarm replied curtly. "Now, stick out your arms so I can get these on you."

As Veeder reluctantly raised his hands, Longarm was aware of the whispered rustle of canvas behind him. He started to turn, but before he could move the cold, steel-hard muzzle of a gun was shoved into the back of his neck.

"Stand real still, Long," a man's voice said. The speaker did not raise his voice above a conversational level, but it was as cold and menacing as the muzzle of his gun. "I've got my finger tight on the trigger, and if you so much as move or blink your eyes, I'll blow your brains out."

Longarm had recognized the voice from its owner's first curt command. It was Zimmerman, and he had seen enough of the Santa Fe superintendent to realize the threat was real.

"I ain't a fool, Zimmerman," he replied, his voice soft. "And I ain't quite ready to die. Tell me what you want me to do and I'll do it."

"All I want you to do right now is stand still," Zimmerman said. He turned to Veeder. "Get rid of these two fellows. Pay 'em off or run 'em away. I don't want anybody in here but us while we're figuring out what to do."

Veeder turned to the wagoneers. "Now, I'm going to double your pay for this trip," he said. "And that extra money's to pay you for keeping your mouths shut. You delivered two steer

carcasses to me this morning. That's all. If you let out a peep
to anybody that you heard or saw anything else, I'll find you,
and if I got to do that, I'll guarantee you'll never say another
word to anybody about anything. *Entiendes?*"

"*Si, Señor Veeder,*" one said, watching Veeder counting
money into his hand. "*Hacemos silencio.*"

"*Comprendemos,*" his companion agreed. "*No dice nada.*"

"Then get the hell outa here," Veeder commanded. "I'll let
you know tomorrow or the next day when to pick up the next
carcass."

After the wagoneers had left, Zimmerman asked Veeder,
"You think they'll do what they said they would?"

"I imagine so. But just in case, I'll have our men up at
Valmora pay 'em a visit and make sure."

"Good idea." Zimmerman turned his full attention back to
Longarm and ordered, "Give your gun to Veeder. Your handcuffs, too. And don't forget to give him the handcuff key at
the same time. I know you've got it in your hand."

Unable to think of any immediate alternative, Longarm
obeyed. Veeder's face broke into an unpleasant grin when he
took Longarm's Colt and pushed it into the waistband of his
pants in order to take the handcuffs. He grabbed them from
Longarm's wrist, where they'd been dangling, and held his
hand out for the key. Longarm let the tiny, flat key drop into
Veeder's hand.

"Well, go ahead and put the cuffs on him, damn it!"
Zimmerman commanded Veeder. "Hurry up! I don't want anybody to walk in and interrupt this little party."

"You got here just in time, Zimmerman," Veeder commented as he put the handcuffs on Longarm's wrists. "I thought
for sure our little deal was going to be finished, and us with
it."

"You underestimated Long," Zimmerman told him. "I made
it my business to find out about him from our railroad police
while I was in Santa Rosa. He's not just any hick-town deputy,
Veeder. He's got a reputation for being smart as well as tough."

"Well, I'm glad to find out what your Santa Fe folks think
about me," Longarm commented, welcoming the opportunity
to say anything that might distract his captors and give him an
opportunity to figure out a way to turn the tables on them.
"Even if I ain't living up to what they told you right now."

"Shut up!" Zimmerman snapped. "I've got a lot of thinking

to do, and I don't need you butting in!"

"What's there to think about?" Veeder asked. "We'll take Long out on the range someplace and shoot him and bury his body. He'll just be marked down as missing, and that'll be the end of him getting in our way."

"I thought you were smarter than that," Zimmerman told Veeder. "This place is crawling with men. The only safe time to get Long off Santa Fe property is at night, when the yard's deserted after the job closes down. And you'll have the crews coming in to eat at noon and supper. How the hell are we going to keep him out of sight until evening?"

"Why, that won't be too hard," Veeder replied. "I've got all sorts of crates around here, and some of 'em are big enough to hold him."

"Drag one up, then," Zimmerman said.

After Veeder had pushed through the tent flap, Longarm said to Zimmerman, "I thought you was a lot smarter than you've turned out to be. I imagine the Santa Fe pays you pretty good. Why'd you get mixed up in the sort of swindle you're pulling?"

"That's not hard to figure out, Long. I'd think you ought to know, after being a lawman so many years."

"Now, there can't be all that much money in dead steers," Longarm said.

"You'd be surprised." The Santa Fe man smiled. "Stop and do a little arithmetic, Long. I've got three hundred men working on this job. That's nearly a thousand meals a day, and they've got to have meat at two of them."

"But them men ain't paying all that much for a meal!"

"As it happens, the Santa Fe's buying their meals because it's one way to keep 'em here and working. Now, you stop to figure it out, day after day, and it adds up to quite a sum."

Longarm shook his head. "I still don't see how it could be worth your while to risk the good job you got on a scheme of that kind. The Santa Fe's sure to catch up with you."

"Hell, they'll never miss it. They're coining money since they opened this new line. And I get a few extra dollars out of waybills that Veeder pays, but he's making enough out of his cut to overlook that."

"It looks to me like you're risking a good job." Longarm frowned.

Zimmerman snorted. "I draw a lot less from the Santa Fe

than I do from my beef deal, Long. Anyhow, going by the Santa Fe rule book, I've got to retire next year, and they're not real generous with their retirement pay."

"Well, I still call it a penny-ante cheating scheme."

Stung, Zimmerman retorted, "Penny-ante, hell! I don't mind telling you, since you won't be around long enough to repeat it, I'm putting away more than two thousand dollars a week, Long. That's a hundred thousand dollars a year, and I imagine you'll agree that's a hell of a lot of money."

Before Longarm could reply, Veeder returned, dragging a large wooden packing case. "This ought to hold him," he said. "I don't expect he'll be in it long enough to get too cramped."

"You're right about that," Zimmerman agreed. "We'll stuff a gag in his mouth and load him into it. Tonight we'll take him out on the range and get rid of him for good. Once he's out of the way, we'll just go on doing business as usual."

Chapter 20

For the hundredth time, it seemed to him, Longarm tried to find a reasonably comfortable position in the packing case. He had lost track of time, but it seemed that he had been squeezed into his present cramped position for an interminable number of hours. He knew it was night, for even though the interior of the box had been dark when its top was first nailed on, there was more density to the darkness now, and the cook-tent had long been silent. Earlier, he'd been able to judge the time by the noises that filtered through the thick boards.

Voices of the workmen from the yards passing on their way to the tables had told Longarm when the noon and evening meals were being served. After both meals he'd heard the voices of the kitchen swampies while they washed dishes and made preliminary preparations for the next meal, but the gag had prevented him from shouting for help. Now, supper had been over long ago, and the help had departed as soon as possible after cleaning up and making a few advance preparations for breakfast. Since then there had been only silence.

Cramped as he was in the big wooden box, Longarm had no way to move in any direction. He had had to fold his knees up to his chin in order to fit into the box. His arms were wrapped around his legs, his handcuffed wrists and hands filling the triangle between his shins and knees. His head was bent forward, resting on his knees. There was no way for him to move more than an inch or two in any direction. His back was bowed, his head bent forward, his feet turned inward at an uncomfortable angle.

You got yourself in a real fix this time, old son, he told himself silently. *Careless, that's what you was. You ought to've known Zimmerman was going to be keeping a close eye on that partner of his. Zimmerman might be a crook, but he sure ain't nobody's fool. You're going to have to do some mighty sharp figuring and some smooth talking to get yourself outa this pickle.*

There being no way to change his situation at the moment, he squirmed around a bit more until he found the position which was the least uncomfortable and settled himself for another period of waiting.

This one was mercifully brief. Longarm heard the soft thud of footsteps. They grew louder and then there was a thunk of a booted foot on the outside of the crate, followed by Zimmerman's voice.

"Quit complaining, Veeder. It's only about a hundred yards to where we left the handcar, and the box isn't all that heavy. We can carry it between us."

"Well, if we're going to do it, let's get on with it," Veeder said. "The sooner we start, the sooner we'll be done."

"All right." There was impatience in Zimmerman's voice. "I'll take this side; you get across from me."

Longarm heard sounds: scraping feet, small noises of hands touching the box. Then one edge tilted sharply upward followed by a cry of protest, and the box dropped back into its original place again.

"Damn it, Veeder! That box came down on my toe!" Zimmerman said angrily. "Put your muscle into it, man! We haven't got all night!"

"I pulled my back outa place when I tried to lift that damn box!" Veeder said. "And I don't care what you say! I'm not having any part of toting it across the yards! We'll open it here and let that son of a bitch walk to the handcar!"

"Well, maybe you're right," Zimmerman agreed. "But don't make any more noise than you have to when you open it."

"Hell, I open these crates every day. I've got my pry-bar right here. I can find it in the dark."

Longarm felt metal thud lightly against the box. Then a sharp bang hit his ears like a thunderclap in the enclosed space and the box shook for a moment. There was a screeching of nails, then a welcome breath of air swept over him as the top of the box swung up. He twisted his head and sat up in spite of the protests of his cramped muscles. In the greater darkness of the cart, the pupils of his eyes had dilated widely and he could see Veeder and Zimmerman almost as clearly as if they had brought a lantern with them.

Veeder stood at one side of the crate, a crowbar in his hand. Zimmerman was standing a bit farther away. He held a double-action Smith & Wesson, its hammer drawn back to full cock, the muzzle pointing unwaveringly at Longarm.

"Take his gag off, Veeder," Zimmerman said. "Maybe we can still make a deal with him." When Veeder had removed the gag, the Santa Fe man went on, "Don't think for a minute that I don't know how to use this, Long. Now, you've got one more chance to be reasonable. I'll make it worth your while—"

"Save your breath, Zimmerman," Longarm broke in. "There ain't any kind of deal I'd make with you. But I'll ask a favor or two of you, if you're inclined to listen."

"I'm not, but go ahead. What is it?"

"First off, I'd like to have my hat. It's all squashed down in the bottom of that box. I feel sorta naked without it."

"You've done me a favor by asking for it," Zimmerman said. "If you hadn't, I might've forgotten about it. Veeder, give him his hat." Veeder found the hat and handed it to Longarm, who began reshaping it before putting it on. Zimmerman went on, "What's the other favor you want, Long?"

"I been in this damn box all day and half the night, and I ain't had a cigar since you closed me into it. Can I get one outa my pocket and light up?"

"Not now, you can't," Zimmerman replied. "But any man who's due to die gets a last request. Wait until we're out of the yards and I'll let you have your smoke."

"I've held out this long. I reckon I can go a bit longer,"

Longarm said. Keeping his voice expressionless, he asked, "I take it you plan to haul me out on the range and kill me?"

"You're partly right. You won't come back alive," Zimmerman replied. His tone was quite casual, as though the subject was unimportant. "Now, I don't want to stay here any longer than we have to. Long, you've been in that box a long time. Can you walk all right?"

"I guess I can make out, even if my legs do feel sorta cramped. Mind telling me where we're headed?"

"You'll find out when we get there," Zimmerman snapped, his voice harder now. "Go on, Veeder, lead the way. Long, you follow him, and I'll be right in back of you. And remember what I said about shooting you."

"I ain't likely to forget," Longarm replied.

He waited until Veeder turned to go and pushed through the tent flap behind him. He did not turn his head to be sure that Zimmerman was following them. He'd seen enough of the Santa Fe man to know that he wasn't the kind to make idle threats.

When he stepped outside the tent, Longarm could tell at once that the hour was very late. The night was clear but moonless, the black sky pierced with the silver pinpoints of countless thousands of stars. Watrous was in almost total darkness; even the light in the town marshal's office was not lighted.

Veeder seemed to know exactly where he was going. He angled across the yards, detouring around the occasional short strings of boxcars that stood on sidings, the heaps of stone ballast where new track was being laid, and the stacks of ties and rails. The walk seemed longer than it actually was. They'd been moving only about five minutes when Veeder stopped beside a handcar that had been lifted off the tracks.

"Help him put the car on the rails, Long," Zimmerman commanded. "Hurry up, now. We've got a ways to go and not much time to waste."

Holding to his role of resignation, Longarm did not protest. He joined Veeder at the handcar and they lifted it onto the tracks, its flanged wheels settling down with a metallic clank.

"Now get aboard," Zimmerman told him. "Sit on one side of the pump-bar."

"Is it all right if I light up now?" Longarm asked.

"We're not out of the yards yet," Zimmerman replied. "You can wait until we get where we're going. But if you'd like to chew on a cigar until you can light it, I won't object. Get one out of his pocket and put it in his mouth, Veeder."

Veeder was standing beside Longarm. He had his hand in motion before Longarm could speak, but instead of his hand going into Longarm's upper vest pocket it went into the lower one.

"Well, I'll be damned!" he exclaimed. "Look what I found in there!"

He held up Longarm's derringer, the watch to which the stubby, wicked-looking little weapon was connected dangling at the other end of the chain that joined them.

"I'll bet you're a pretty good poker player, Long," Zimmerman remarked. "You didn't act one bit like you had an ace in the hole."

"Looks like you're holding all the cards now, Zimmerman," Longarm said calmly. "But there might be another deal coming up that'll change my luck."

"Don't count on it," Zimmerman replied dryly. "Remember, I'm the one who's dealing."

Veeder had been handling the derringer, feeling its smooth walnut burl butt and the satiny finish of its barrel. "This'll be a nice souvenir for me," he said.

"And you'll get to keep it until we get where we're going," Zimmerman snapped. "Damn it, don't you know Long's got to have it on his body when they find him?"

"I hadn't thought about that," Veeder replied.

"Well, start thinking for a change! Now, get on the handcar, Long. Veeder, let's shove it off. You get on in front, I'll take the back."

Longarm realized argument or efforts to delay would be useless. He sat down on the deck of the handcar. Zimmerman and Veeder pushed it ahead, then jumped on and began pumping the handles. After a few minutes, they caught the rhythm needed in their pumping and the little vehicle gained speed. They rolled through the night at a good clip.

As the few lights of Watrous dimmed and disappeared, the Santa Fe boss said to Longarm, "All right, you can light up now. Nobody's apt to be around here to see a cigar burning."

Longarm took out a cheroot and match and succeeded in lighting the long, thin cigar on his first try. The wind that the moving handcar was creating roiled the smoke as Zimmerman and Veeder rocked up and down on the crossbarred handle. They rode in silence for perhaps a quarter of an hour before either of them spoke.

Then Zimmerman called to his partner in crime. "Take it slow now, Veeder. The place we're looking for is just a little way ahead."

Longarm glanced along the tracks and saw that they curved just ahead of the handcar. He had an idea of the fate Zimmerman and Veeder had planned for him, but he said nothing. The handcar was barely making headway now as his captors slowed the rhythm of their pumping.

"Stop right here!" Zimmerman exclaimed. "The engineer of a train can't see far enough ahead to put on the brakes in time to stop before he's past this spot when the engine's started into that curve up there."

Metal squealed on metal as Veeder stamped on the brake and the handcar slowed and stopped. He and Zimmerman dropped to the ground and stood gazing through the darkness up the track. Longarm's eyes followed theirs. He could see the sweep of the rails as they curved ahead and realized the fate his captors had planned for him. He sat motionless and said nothing, his mind busy making his own plans.

"All right, Long," Zimmerman said as he and Veeder started back to the handcar. "This is as far as you go. Get off the car and let's get set."

"I don't see as I owe you two any help," Longarm replied, his voice mild. "You wanta put me across the tracks, it's going to be up to you to carry me."

Zimmerman was only an arm's length away by now. He drew his revolver, pushed it into Longarm's throat, and snarled, "The way you'll look by the time that train runs over you, nobody's going to notice a bullet hole. Now, you can live a few minutes longer and try to figure out how to get away, or you can die right now. It's up to you."

"Well, when you put it that way, I guess I might as well go along," Longarm said, standing up.

"That's better," Zimmerman snapped. He stepped behind Longarm and shoved the revolver muzzle into his back. "March up the tracks till I tell you to stop. Veeder, get the cuffs ready."

Longarm had taken only half a dozen steps before Zimmerman called for him to halt. "Shove one end of those cuffs between the bottom of the rail and the ballast, Veeder. Long, you lay belly-down down on the ballast. We'll get you set later."

Longarm had foreseen Zimmerman's plan almost as soon as they started for the handcar. He lay face-down on the rough stones that ballasted the rails, and made no objection when Veeder snapped the shackles on his wrists.

"Haul his feet outside the rail and weight them down with a pile of ballast," Zimmerman told Veeder. "We want the wheels to tear him up as bad as possible." He waited until his partner in crime had obeyed, then went on, "Now, put that derringer and his watch back in his vest pockets." While Veeder was working, Zimmerman took Longarm's Colt out of his belt and restored it to its holster.

Turning his head as far as the handcuffs and his weighted feet would allow him to, Longarm said over his shoulder, "Looks like you figured everything out, Zimmerman. But you missed the only thing that'd make it perfect."

"What's that?" Zimmerman asked. "You'll have your gun, your derringer, and your badge. When the crew of that train scrapes you up, they won't find anything to ask questions about."

"Except how come I got handcuffs on," Longarm replied.

"Oh, I'll take care of that," Zimmerman promised. "The train crew won't stay here but a few minutes. They'll have to get to Watrous on schedule. I'll be the one who handles the investigation of your unfortunate death in an unavoidable accident." He paused, then added, "But I'll tell you this, Long. You're sure taking this like a man."

"Oh, I don't figure I'm done for yet," Longarm replied calmly. "I don't know how much time I'll have before that next train's due, but I've got outa worse scrapes before. Don't be surprised, later on, when I come looking for you to arrest you and your partner."

"Now, that's just blather!" Veeder exclaimed. "You won't be arresting nobody after tonight, Long! Me and Zimmerman have fixed it up so there's not a hole anybody can find to get to us. Ain't that right, Zimmerman?"

"There's only one hole that's left, Veeder," Zimmerman replied. "And I'm closing it up right now."

"What're you talking—" Veeder began.

His words were cut off by the crack of Zimmerman's revolver as the Santa Fe man raised the weapon and shot Veeder through the heart.

"I'm sure you understand why I had to do that," Zimmerman said calmly. His voice was as casually conversational as though he were explaining why he wanted coffee after dinner.

"Sure," Longarm replied. "Veeder was a talker."

"You're very acute, Marshal Long," Zimmerman said. He dragged Veeder's corpse across the road ballast and pulled it across Longarm's prone form. He straightened up and went on, "I don't think there'll be any loopholes left that I can't plug. Goodbye, Long. It's too bad you're so damned honest. I'd like very much to've had you for my partner instead of Veeder."

"Don't put too much store in saying goodbye," Longarm said as Zimmerman started toward the handcar. "I'll be coming after you in a little while."

Zimmerman did not reply. In a moment Longarm heard the rasping of the handcar's pump-lever and the grinding of its wheel flanges on the tracks. When the sound had died away completely, he began the unpleasant task that lay ahead.

Kicking his legs as best he could under the weight of Veeder's limp body, he got rid of the gravel that weighted down his feet. Then he dug the toes of his boots into the roadbed and began pushing himself forward.

Veeder's dead weight made the job long and difficult, but Longarm was persistent. He ignored the scratches inflicted on his knees and thighs by the sharp-edged gravel of the ballast, and shoved himself forward inch by inch until he had created a bit of slack in the chain connecting the handcuffs.

He was still moving ahead when he heard the whistle of the oncoming train, but the sound did not panic him. He dropped his head until the brim of his hat touched his hands. Taking off the hat, he began feeling inside the leather sweatband for the spare handcuff key he always carried there. By the time he found it, the rails were humming, and he could see the glow of the train's headlamp around the curve.

Get a move on, old son! Longarm told himself silently as he groped for the keyhole in his manacles. *That engine's going to be on you in just about two more minutes!*

Working by feel, hampered by the short length of chain that remained after it had been passed under the rail, he finally found the keyhole of the cuff on his left hand. The train whistled the curve again, its headlamp now a bright swathe in the darkness, as the handcuff fell away from his left wrist.

Taking the key in his free hand, Longarm unlocked the other cuff. With both hands free, he made quick work of ridding himself of the encumbrance of Veeder's body. He finally succeeded in pushing it aside to roll off the tracks and down the low grade before diving to safety himself as the engine rounded the curve and bathed him in its light.

Brakes squealed and rasped with a grinding of metal scraping metal. Steam spurted from the engine's pistons and sent up a cloud that shrouded the area. Couplings clashed with a series of explosive bangings. The cars telescoped into one another as the engineer and fireman brought the train to a scraping halt. The inertia of the cars pushed the locomotive and tender fifty yards down the tracks from where Longarm stood.

Longarm kept his position instead of walking to meet the brakeman who leaped from the baggage car and the engineer and fireman who tumbled out of the locomotive and started racing back beside the cars. The lantern carried by the brakeman bobbed furiously as they ran.

He heard gravel scraping down the string of cars and peered back. Even in the faint light, he could see the glint of the badge on the conductor's cap as he ran beside the cars. Longarm took a cigar from his vest pocket. It was bent, and he carefully worked it straight before lighting it.

"What the hell's going on here?" the engineer shouted even before he and his companions reached Longarm's side.

Longarm waited a few seconds until the conductor had reached the scene, then held up his badge for them to see by the light of the brakeman's lantern. He said, "My name's Long, deputy U.S. marshal outa the Denver office. I need you men to give me a hand while I close up a case I been working on."

"But what about—" the conductor began.

Longarm broke in and said, "I ain't got time to explain all of it now." He turned to the conductor and went on, "You're in charge, the railroad rules say. Suppose you just tell everybody to go along with what I need for you to do. I guarantee you men won't get into no trouble with your bosses."

"I've heard your name before, Marshal Long," the conductor said. "You're the one they call Longarm." He nodded to the engine crew and went on, "Do what he says. I don't think we'll be sorry."

• • •

Following Longarm's instructions, the engineer began blowing the whistle as the locomotive rolled into the Watrous yards. A light glowed inside the office-tent. When the whistle broke the night, the brakeman put a carefully measured pressure on the brake lever to bring the engine to a halt beside the tent.

Zimmerman came rushing out, stopped beside the cab, and called to the engineer, "What's wrong? You're not scheduled to stop here!"

Longarm swung around the end of the tender, let go of the grab-bar, and dropped to the roadbed. Zimmerman turned when he heard Longarm's feet scraping on the gravel.

"You—you're not—damn it! You can't be—" Zimmerman began, then began clawing for the butt of his holstered pistol.

Longarm's draw was faster and his aim was true. Zimmerman buckled when the Colt's slug cut through his heart, then started crumpling. Longarm walked past the sprawled body without looking at it, and waved to the engine crew to move on. The engineer pushed the throttle forward and the train slowly picked up speed.

In the darkness that shrouded the scene after the train lights faded, Longarm glanced at the dark, huddled form beside the tracks. He took out a cheroot and lighted it. The fitful night breeze had died away by now, and the white smoke wreathed his head.

"It ain't right for one man to be judge and jury both, I reckon," he said aloud. "But this damn case was so mixed up that if it ever got to court a jury likely couldn't've made heads or tails of it. Now all that's left is a coroner's inquest, and Pleas O'Neal can handle them while you head back to Denver."

Longarm started walking slowly toward the town, where a light still glowed in the marshal's office. He took out his watch and held it up to let the coal on his cigar light the face. He began smiling when he saw the hour.

"And after you get through explaining things to Pleas, old son, there'll still be time for you to drop in and say goodbye to that nice little Beth Whiting."

Watch for

LONGARM AND THE CROOKED RAILMAN

ninety-second novel in the bold
LONGARM series, and

**LONGARM AND THE LONE STAR
SHOWDOWN**

the next GIANT LONGARM adventure
featuring the LONE STAR duo

coming in August from Jove!

Explore the exciting Old West with
one of the men who made it wild!